Thankful for Love

PEGGY BIRD

CRIMSON
ROMANCE

F+W Media, Inc.

Published by
Crimson Romance
an imprint of F+W Media, Inc.
10151 Carver Road, Suite 200
Blue Ash, OH 45242. U.S.A.
www.crimsonromance.com

ISBN 10: 1-4405-9500-3
ISBN 13: 978-1-4405-9500-4
eISBN 10: 1-4405-9498-8
eISBN 13: 978-1-4405-9498-4

Cover art ©iStockphoto.com/Moncherie.

First, this book is dedicated to Ben, one of the best grandsons anyone could have. When you're old enough to read it, you'll see how much of you I borrowed to create Lucas.

Second, I want to thank Melody Miller, sales director for the Wildhorse Resort and Casino on the Umatilla Reservation, who let me pick her brain about life in the area. If I got it right, she was a good teacher. If I got it wrong, I was a bad student.

Last, I owe thanks to the people of Crow Agency and the Rocky Boy's Reservation. Two years working as a public health nurse on those reservations taught this East Coast girl much about dignity, tradition, and pride.

Chapter 1

Jack Richardson knew what was coming as soon as Anne Salazar said, "We need to talk." He even felt a sense of relief that it was finally happening.

"I'm listening, Anne," he said.

She put on her jacket as she spoke, avoiding looking directly at him, paying more attention to buttoning it up than she needed to. "I can't do this anymore. I'm so, so sorry, but I can't." When she finally looked up at him, he saw regret in her eyes. He was sure she saw the same in his.

"I'm not surprised. I've been wearing you out with what I've needed from you," he said. He reached for her hand, but she didn't respond to his gesture.

"I've been only too happy to help. I love you. You know I do. But I'm…"

"Done with it?"

"I'd stay if I could. But this body of mine isn't what it used to be. I'm seventy. I need to have my hip replaced. I can't take care of two active boys while I'm in the hospital and at PT appointments."

"You don't need to apologize. I understand. You've been the best grandmother and mother-in-law anyone could ask for. I don't know what the boys and I would have done without you after Paula died."

Tears appeared at the mention of the death of her daughter—Jack's wife—from ovarian cancer two and a half years ago. "I wanted to help. Had to help or I'd have gone crazy. I hate to leave you in the lurch like this, but the doc says I shouldn't put it off any longer."

Jack hugged her. "We'll be fine. I'll start looking tomorrow for someone to help. When's the surgery?"

"Not for a month, so you have a little time." She patted her son-in-law on the arm. "I'm not sure what I'll miss the most—feeling like I'm helping you out or being a part of my grandsons' lives."

"You make it sound like you're moving to Timbuktu. You'll still be part of their lives."

"But not every day the way I've been since ... well, for the past couple years."

Anxious to assure her she wouldn't be losing touch with her grandsons, Jack said, "When you're back on your feet, we'll work something out so you see them regularly. Don't worry about it. Get yourself taken care of."

Anne gathered up her purse and several containers, now empty of the food she'd brought over to feed the three Richardson males. "Shall I tell the boys, or do you want to?"

"How about we both do it? When I've got someone else lined up, we'll tell them together. Fair enough?"

"More than fair." She put her arms around his waist in a farewell hug. "I wish I didn't have to do this."

"We can't have you working so hard you end up on the DL. Don would shoot me." Don was Anne's husband, the kids' grandfather.

"He wouldn't shoot you, although he might make your life a living hell at family dinners." She gave him a kiss on his cheek and released him. "You've looked out for everyone else for so long you haven't had a chance to do anything for yourself. And now I've made it even harder for you."

"You haven't. I'll be fine." Jack accompanied her to the door then watched her walk slowly to her car. The limp he'd begun to notice a few months back was more pronounced. Either it was worse or she was no longer trying to hide the pain. Whichever it was, it was why he hadn't been surprised at her announcement.

He was glad she was getting her hip taken care of, but he had to admit it did make his life more complicated. It was spring. The wheat on his Eastern Oregon ranch was beginning to produce heads of grain and needed attention. He had to get the rest of the alfalfa he'd use to feed his small herd of cattle over the winter planted. The same herd of cattle that had begun calving. Then there was the foal due from the mare his late wife had loved.

Now he had to add finding someone to help with kid wrangling. At the rate things were going, he'd be an old, old man before he'd have a chance to do what Anne suggested—find time for himself.

• • •

"Any extra shifts for me this week?" Quanna Morales asked her supervisor. "I'll even work a double."

"Sorry, kiddo, but unless someone calls in sick, I've got all the slots filled. Will you be around if I need you at the last minute?"

"I'm working the breakfast and lunch shift at the resort this weekend, but I'm available otherwise. You know how to find me."

"Believe me, if I need you, I'll find you. You're the most dependable part-timer on staff."

Her shift as an aide at the Golden Years Retirement Community over, Quanna headed for home with nothing to do for the rest of the day except fret about money. And how, if she didn't make more soon, she'd have to move back to the Umatilla Reservation where she'd grown up.

When she'd left for Portland so she could follow her dream of being a teacher, she had assumed that by the time she was in her late twenties, she'd be back on the rez in another way—teaching kids who needed to see that they, too, could have their dreams come true. But her life had unfolded a little differently than she had planned. The cost of living in the city and paying tuition was more than she'd imagined, so she'd had to recalculate how long it would take to get her degree. Then, about three years ago, her father died of a sudden heart attack, leaving her mother with few resources to take care of Miguel, her brother who'd been born with Down syndrome and several heart problems. She and her siblings had to pitch in. Quanna was the only unmarried one.

So she volunteered to move back over the mountains to help financially and to be available to stay with her brother to give her mother some respite.

The two part-time jobs she'd patched together since coming back—her job at the retirement home as well as a shift every now and then at the restaurant in the resort on the rez—made it almost possible to afford her tiny apartment, a class at the local community college, and her contribution to her brother's care. The operative word being "almost." If something didn't change, she would have to move back in with her mother if she had any shot at achieving her goal of finishing her degree so she could teach.

With everything on her mind, the sunny day and the sweet, sage-y smells of spring in the high plains didn't lift her spirits the way they usually did. She was merely reminded by what was around her that another season had arrived with little progress toward her goals.

• • •

"I was glad to see you were working today," Quanna's friend Rita said when Quanna got to work in the middle of the following week. "I was afraid you'd miss out on the hot cowboy's usual visit to Joan Anthony." Rita was almost drooling as she glanced up and down the hall.

Of course Quanna knew who Rita meant. Every woman in the place knew the guy. Mrs. Anthony had once described him as a nephew who was more like a son. Most of the female staff described him as yummy.

He was older, probably in his mid-forties, and he was a real deal cowboy, not the "big hat, no cattle" kind. His boots were made for work not show, and for the clincher, he sported a Stetson tan in the summer—pale forehead, where his hat rode low, the rest of his face dark from the sun. His jeans, which fit like they'd been tailored for him, were what the staff appreciated most. Well, his tight Wrangler butt the jeans showed off.

His sandy brown hair always looked a little shaggy, and his deep chocolate eyes looked sad until he smiled and crinkles appeared around them to complement the dimples in his cheeks. He looked like he was in great shape and walked with the assurance of a man who was comfortable in his skin.

But there was something a little mysterious in the expression on his face, like he was holding something back. It was sexy and made all the women who drooled over him want to comfort him. Or something.

During his visits to Joan Anthony, some of the aides had been known to "drop by" her apartment to she if she needed anything just to get into a conversation with him. He was charming and funny, and they hoped by talking to him, they could uncover his secret, whatever it was. Quanna hadn't resorted to such an extreme. But she had asked Mrs. Anthony about him.

His name was Jack Richardson, and he ran a wheat operation twenty-five miles outside Pendleton. His late father was Mrs. Anthony's brother.

Today, however, instead of going directly to his aunt's apartment, Richardson went to the director's office. The staff gossip was hot and heavy about whether this meant Mrs. Anthony was about to be moved out of the facility or, if she stayed, transferred from independent to assisted living. She had, after all, been showing signs of slowing down recently, beginning to have trouble with some of the activities of daily living. Maybe her family had decided it was time to upgrade her level of care. The women all hoped she would be staying. She was one of the nicest people they cared for, and they would miss her. Not to mention miss seeing the hot cowboy.

Turned out, what he was apparently doing was asking permission to put a flier on the staff bulletin board before he went to see his aunt. Curious, Quanna took a look at what he posted the first chance she could. It was an advertisement for a job at the Richardson ranch, a "kid wrangler," as it was described, for two young boys, with additional light housekeeping and cooking duties. The job was full time. The pay worked out to be double the hourly rate she was making at the retirement facility. Although she had no childcare experience other than babysitting when she was a teenager, Quanna was sure she could craft her résumé to show she had the skills needed. This could be the answer to her money problems. If only there were some way to ensure she had the inside track for the job.

Maybe there was. At the bottom of the flier were tear-off bits of paper with a phone number and e-mail address on each piece. Looking around to make sure no one was watching, she carefully tore off all but two of the pieces. She wanted the job. If it took cheating to get it, she was willing to do it.

Instead of going home at the end of her shift that day, Quanna waited in the parking lot for the cowboy to appear. Feeling like she was stalking him—because, face it, she was—she followed him and watched where he posted more fliers. When he headed out of town, she returned to each place and removed most of the tear-off tags from the fliers. She didn't think it was smart to remove them all. He'd think it odd if she was the only person who contacted him about the job.

But she would make sure she was one of only a handful. That would lower the odds of someone more qualified getting the job she already thought of as hers. At least, she hoped it would.

Chapter 2

Panic didn't set in until Quanna was on her way to the Richardson Ranch for her interview. She'd been calm all through her preparations—choosing from her very limited wardrobe the nicest clothes she owned, taking pains to make sure she looked neat and tidy, carefully putting the hard copies of her references in a file folder so they wouldn't get crumpled, organizing the sample menus highlighting her meal planning and cooking skills. Armed with enough paperwork to apply for a job with Homeland Security and ready to nail the interview, she left Pendleton in plenty of time to make her two-thirty appointment.

Then, about halfway there, the doubts she'd had off and on since she'd applied for the job reemerged. She'd barely hung up from the phone call arranging the interview when she had begun to wonder if her excitement about the salary and stability of the position had clouded her judgment. After all, what did she know about this man or his situation? Maybe in spite of his good manners, he didn't like Indians. She'd known more than one local rancher who didn't. Maybe he was a misogynistic jerk who'd treat her badly. She'd be alone in his home, isolated on a ranch miles away from Pendleton, with only two kids as company. Or witnesses.

In her panic, she had turned to the only person she knew who might have some answers—Joan Anthony—and asked about him, explaining why she wanted to know. What she got in response was a long hymn of praise for Jack Richardson.

Mrs. Anthony said her nephew was the most responsible and levelheaded member of a family with deep roots in the community. When his parents were killed in a plane crash, it was Jack who had sacrificed his college career to finish raising his younger brother and run the family ranch. He'd lost his wife to cancer two years ago and was now raising the two sons they'd struggled to have through years of fertility problems. The job he was trying to fill had until recently been done by his mother-in-law who had been helping out since the death of his wife.

The Richardson Ranch was not one of the biggest in the county, Joan Anthony had said, although it was one of the oldest land grants. She bragged that the current generation of Richardsons was the fourth to work the land, with the fifth already living there. Quanna had held her tongue and didn't say some of her ancestors had been there centuries before there *was* a county.

Jack's backstory helped explain the sadness in his eyes, although the image of sainthood Mrs. Anthony had painted sounded a bit overblown. On the other hand, he did seem a decent enough guy when he visited his aunt. He was attentive and polite, all "yes, ma'am" and "no, ma'am." All "please" and "if you have time" with everyone. He was respectful to staff, never treating Quanna or anyone else who was an underling or a minority differently than he treated the director. He didn't seem to be the kind of person who'd make snide comments about her Indian/Latina blood, the way some of her coworkers did. The same coworkers who routinely hit on her. He didn't seem like the sort who'd do that either.

Even if he wasn't as saintly as Joan Anthony described, he was obviously someone who had earned the respect of a woman Quanna knew was a savvy judge of people. Still, her level of anxiety had risen and fallen like the tide the closer she got to the day of her interview.

It was now at full flood as she drove to the Richardson Ranch. Finally, her head was calmed by what she saw outside her car—the seemingly endless expanse of the Eastern Oregon high plains she was driving through. She loved the landscape, even the scrubland where nothing would ever thrive except the ubiquitous tumbleweed. The land, her homeland, had always soothed her, even when she was a kid, and it did now. She lowered the window in her car and inhaled the smells of sage and warm earth and growing wheat.

The year's crop wasn't even hip-high yet, but it looked healthy. Green stalks, which were beginning to produce heads of grain, moved with the slightest breeze, making it seem they were waving to her in a friendly and welcoming way.

In the distance, she could see a dozen head of cattle. Hardly anyone in Umatilla County made a living on cattle anymore, but some ranchers still ran a small herd. Mostly it was for their own consumption, although some sold designer beef to white tablecloth restaurants in the trendy neighborhoods of Portland or to the upscale markets that liked to advertise who raised their ribs and roasts.

The more likely source of income for the ranches and farms she was passing were the wind turbines occasionally seen on the hills, slowly turning, generating power for California. The huge white generators kept a number of family operations in the black with rental payments for the land on which they were built.

The directions to the ranch were easy to follow—right after the milepost twenty-five marker was a two story high, whitewashed gate composed of huge side logs and a cross beam from which hung two Rs, one reversed so the letters were back to back. The place was called simply the Richardson Ranch. No phony Spanish or fancy, cutesy name. A straightforward explanation of where you were.

The dirt road off the main highway went for a number of miles before dipping down into a small hollow where three hills came close to intersecting. On the crest of the hills, wind turbines presided over the scene below.

As Quanna drove down the hill, she saw the darker green of trees interspersed with buildings. One, a big red building, was obviously a barn, big enough to hold quite a few horses or head of cattle. There were several smaller red structures grouped around it where farm equipment was probably stored.

Set at some distance from the barn complex was the ranch house. Joan Anthony had told her it had been built over time by succeeding generations of Richardsons who renovated, rebuilt, and added to the small one-room cabin put up by the original rancher. After all those years, it had morphed into a two-story, stately looking residence with a deep-set porch running the entire front of the house. Painted white with sage green shutters on the upstairs windows, the house was protected from the weather by large junipers, cottonwoods, and pine trees, which, judging from their size, had been planted decades ago.

Parked outside the house was a dusty, white Ford pickup truck with an extended cab, the kind her brother had always wanted to own but could never afford. It didn't look brand new, but it looked well cared for. Next to it was a Toyota sedan. Quanna parked the old Honda her brother had loaned her on a more or less permanent basis beside the sedan, steadied herself with a couple deep breaths, and went to meet what she hoped was her future.

An older woman answered her knock. "Oh, you're early. I didn't expect you yet."

It wasn't exactly the welcome she'd hoped for and only increased her nervousness. "I'm sorry. Do you want me to wait in the car until it's time?"

"No, no. Come in. It's fine." She led Quanna into a large, light-filled living room. "I'm Anne Salazar, Jack's mother-in-law."

Quanna extended her hand. "I'm Quanna Morales."

Anne seemed to hesitate for a few seconds before taking the outstretched hand. "Jack's on the phone. Something about part of the irrigation system not working right. He'll be with us in a minute." She waved her hand toward a set of sofas covered in a beige fabric and two oversized leather armchairs. "Take a seat wherever you're comfortable," she said. "Can I get you a glass of water?"

Quanna sat on the edge of the seat of one of the armchairs. "That would be nice, thank you."

While the woman was in the kitchen, Quanna looked around the room. If she'd had a dream house, it would look a lot like this one. It was like something out of a magazine.

The room where she was sitting was probably the original part of the house if the floor-to-ceiling, freestanding stone fireplace dominating the middle of the room was any indication. On a rough-hewn wooden mantle was a display of what she assumed were family photos, most of them featuring the man she knew from Golden Years, a beautiful blonde woman, or two boys. To the right of the fireplace, a set of stairs led to the upper story. Behind it was a door open enough for her to see a room with more couches and chairs and the corner of what she suspected was a large television set.

To the left of the fireplace was a door leading to another room—a dining room, maybe? Another door at the far left, through which Mrs. Salazar had disappeared, was, she supposed, the kitchen. At the other end of the room, tucked under the staircase, was a baby grand piano, the lid down, the bench pushed under the keyboard.

On the walls were paintings depicting Eastern Oregon landscapes in all four seasons. Pillows covered in traditional striped Pendleton woolen fabrics were tossed on the sofas. No rugs obscured any part of the wide boards of the hardwood floors. The overall effect was casual, comfortable, and beautiful.

Mrs. Salazar returned with a glass full of ice, a bottle of mineral water, and Jack Richardson. He was holding a cell phone and frowning.

Quanna started to rise, but he waved her off, the frown disappearing as he acknowledged her.

"Please, don't stand. You'll make me feel like the old man I'm afraid I'm turning into." He enveloped her hand in his. His handshake was a warm grip of a large, strong, slightly calloused hand. She liked the feel of it and was surprised to find how much she enjoyed touching him. She immediately dismissed her reaction as inappropriate.

"I recognize you now," he said. "I couldn't put a face to your name when we talked on the phone. All I remembered was how much Aunt Joan likes you. You're one of her favorites. She's always praising you." He grinned, and the room seemed to get a bit brighter and warmer. "Actually, I'm not sure I should be interviewing you for this job. I don't know what she'll say if I steal you away from Golden Years."

The panic Quanna felt at his comment must have shown on her face because he quickly added, "I'm joking. She called this morning to tell me she can't think of anyone better suited to the job than you."

"That was kind of her, Mr. Richardson. I didn't ask her to."

"Jack, please. And the first thing she told me was you didn't know she was calling." The smile got wider. "She also said you asked her about me."

Quanna could feel her face heat up. "I didn't mean to be disrespectful, I just..."

"You wanted to make sure of what you were getting into," he interrupted. "I'd have done the same thing."

Jack settled back into the couch. "Hope you don't mind. I asked Anne to sit in on the interview. She's been my kid wrangler for a couple years now. She can probably give you a better idea of what the job entails than I can. She can also warn you about working here. Apparently, it leads to the need to have your hip replaced."

Anne slapped him lightly on the hand but didn't make a comment on his joking reference to her ailment.

"Of course I don't mind," Quanna said.

"Okay, then let's get started," Jack said. "I'd like to get the formal part out of the way before the boys get home from school.

Tell me why you want this job and how your experience makes you a good candidate for it."

• • •

Maybe because his kids' grandmother had been taking care of the boys, Jack had thought of a kid wrangler as middle-aged, at least. But only one of the handful of applicants he'd heard from was past forty. And she was older than Anne and even less able to get around.

Quanna, like the rest of the few who'd responded to his fliers, was young. Like the others, she was, to his forty-four-year-old eyes, almost a kid. Although she was not as young as the other two he'd interviewed. They were barely out of high school, with little experience in managing their own lives, let alone someone else's. One of them admitted she'd be leaving for college as soon as she saved enough money, meaning he'd have to look for her replacement in the near future. He suspected both of them would leave in a heartbeat if they found anything more interesting to them.

Quanna, on the other hand, had real life experience holding a steady job. And he'd heard she was good. Not only from the manager of the Golden Years facility, her former boss in Portland, and her supervisor at the restaurant at the casino resort on the reservation but also from his aunt.

Seeing her close up now, he registered for the first time how pretty she was. She had dark brown eyes, copper brown skin, and thick, shiny black hair she wore in one long, loose braid that hung over her right shoulder. When he'd seen her before, she'd been in baggy scrubs. Now she was in jeans and a knit shirt and looked more like a teenager than a woman in her late twenties, which he guessed she was from the information about her work life on her résumé.

Obviously looks weren't on his list of requirements for a kid wrangler, but it wouldn't be the worst thing to have an attractive woman around the house again.

Now, as she spoke enthusiastically about her work experience in her jobs in Pendleton and Portland and how it had prepared her to take care of his kids, her calm, competent manner convinced him—she might be the answer to his problem. If she could figure out what to do about the foul-up in the irrigation system, he'd nominate her for sainthood.

His divergence to his other problem had taken his mind out of the interview. His inattention was apparently obvious. Anne was looking oddly at him, and Quanna seemed to be waiting for him to say something.

"I'm sorry. I've been distracted all morning with a problem in the fields." He leaned forward and picked up the papers she had placed on the coffee table. Rifling through them, he said, "I've talked to your references, which were even more glowing on the phone than they were in writing. You're obviously qualified. So, why don't you ask me—or Anne—what you want to know about the job?"

Quanna asked about hours, the probability of weekend work, how late she'd be expected to stay on school days, what the arrangements were for school holidays and vacations. She asked about his sons' eating habits and if she'd be expected to provide transportation to and from afterschool activities.

She asked so many questions, they hadn't gotten in a tour of the house when the front door flew open and two boys, all legs, arms, and energy, ran into the entryway. Both looked like carbon copies of Jack with sandy-colored hair and brown eyes. Both looked curiously at the woman sitting on the edge of her seat in the living room.

"Hey, guys," Jack said. "Shoes off. Books on the bench. Then come meet someone." When they had done as he asked, he introduced them. "Quanna, this is Daniel and his younger brother, Lucas. Daniel's ten, and Lucas is eight. Boys, this is Quanna Morales. She's applied for the job of keeping you two from living on junk food and wrecking the house." He nodded at them, and as he'd taught them, they shook hands with her.

"Hello," Daniel said, his expression guarded, as it always was when he was introduced to new people or situations.

"Hi," Lucas said. He cocked his head to one side. "You have a funny name."

"Don't be rude," Jack said at the same time Anne said, "Lucas!"

"It's okay. I get that all the time," Quanna said. "Yes, it's unusual, isn't it? It's Indian. My mother is Umatilla and is an admirer of Quanah Parker, who was a famous Indian leader. She changed the spelling of his name a little, but that's who I'm named for. His parents were white and Indian. I'm mixed culturally, too. My dad was born in Central America."

"My teacher grew up on the reservation," Lucas said.

"I did, too. Maybe I know her."

"Her name's Ms. Eagleman."

"Mary? I know her and her family." Quanna said. "So, what's your favorite thing she teaches?"

In a rather theatrical fashion, using his body as he talked, Lucas explained his struggle with math and science and his love for words and the arts. When Quanna asked Daniel the same question, he answered less dramatically, saying that he did well in most subjects but, unlike his brother, liked science best.

"Good, then maybe you can help me with my homework when I'm having trouble," Quanna said.

"Grown-ups don't have homework," Lucas said.

"This one does," she answered. "I take classes sometimes at Blue Mountain, and I've been taking a lot of science classes lately."

Jack watched the interchange between Quanna and his sons with growing pleasure. She wasn't condescending or uptight. She talked to them with genuine interest and respect. She listened to what they said before she responded. Lucas appeared to be warming to her already, although Daniel, as he would have expected, looked like he was reserving judgment.

Her references had obviously not been an exaggeration. Her qualifications were perfect, even if her experience was working with adults, not kids. If the conversation she was having right now was any indication, she didn't have any trouble connecting with children.

She was clearly the most qualified applicant he'd had, although that didn't say much. It had puzzled him when so few people had called him for information about the job. Of course, after this interview, he realized Quanna was more than just the most qualified in a group of mostly marginal applicants—she would have been outstanding in any field of job seekers.

But what really sealed the deal was Aunt Joan's recommendation. He didn't know if Quanna appreciated it, but having his aunt vouch for her was pure gold.

Aunt Joan had saved his mental, if not physical, life when he'd had to take over running the ranch after his parents died. She helped him deal with the guilt he'd felt because his father had been piloting his plane over the Cascade Mountains so they could visit Jack at Oregon State when they crashed. She gave him guidance on how to cope with his teenaged brother, as well as manage the family's wheat operation to keep it from slowly sinking into debt. She even referred him to the outfit looking for land on which to put their wind turbines. The company had saved them. He hated how their giant white monsters broke up the landscape but loved what they did to his bottom line.

After his aunt's phone call, he'd been almost ready to hire Quanna Morales as soon as she walked in. Now, with her earnest explanation of why she wanted the job, some of which he'd actually heard, her careful prep for the interview, complete with relevant questions and menus, for God's sake, and her immediate interest in Daniel and Lucas, he was sure.

"Sorry to interrupt, boys, but Quanna and I still have some things to discuss. Your grandmother left a snack in the kitchen for you. Then you better get to your homework. And don't forget your chores in the barn before dinner."

The two children politely said goodbye and disappeared into the kitchen. When they were gone, Jack said, "Quanna, before we talk more, maybe it would be a good idea for Anne to show you around the house and give you a chance to ask her questions about how she's been handling things. I'll get the boys settled in the dining room and meet you back here in, what, fifteen minutes?" He looked at Anne for confirmation. She nodded. "See you then."

• • •

It was the most beautiful house Quanna had ever been in. The kitchen was well laid out with new-ish, stainless steel appliances, including twin ovens and an oversized refrigerator. There was a decent-sized eating island in the middle of the room. Off the back of the kitchen, a hall led to a mudroom, a small shower and powder room, and the door out to the barn complex.

Upstairs were four bedrooms, a small home office, and a laundry room. Each boy had a room with bunk beds. They shared a bath with each other and with the guest room. The master bedroom had an en suite bath with a large shower. Pendleton blankets were everywhere.

Anne answered all her questions, pointed out the oddities of each room, showed her where the boys hid things when they were supposed to have cleaned up their rooms. She asked a few questions of her own, too, seeming to be skeptical both about Quanna's ability to manage two active boys and her interest in staying with the job over time. From the encouraging way the interview had gone downstairs, Quanna had thought she had a good shot at getting the job. Now she wondered if she had been too optimistic. If this woman had anything to say about it, her chances weren't good.

Between Anne's questions and Quanna's, it was more like twenty-five minutes before they made it back to the living room.

"Well," Jack began. "What do you think?"

"Your home is beautiful," she answered.

"I appreciate the compliment, but I meant do you think you can manage the job?"

"Oh, yes. I'm sure I can." She fought back the urge to ask if he'd please, please hire her.

As if he'd heard her plea, he said, "Then you're hired."

After her conversation upstairs with Anne Salazar, the offer of the job came with a feeling of relief. It also came with an urge to throw her arms around her new boss's neck so she could hug him—an impulse wildly unsuitable at a job interview but somehow enticing. "Thank you so much. You have no idea what this means to me, to my family. When do you want me to start?"

"You'll want to give notice at Golden Years, I imagine. And Anne's not scheduled for surgery for two weeks. How 'bout you start in a week? You'll have a week to overlap with her to get used to the house before we leave you to wrangle my kids all by yourself. That work for you?"

She barely remembered saying yes, shaking hands with Anne and Mr. Richardson—ah, Jack—saying good-bye to Daniel and Lucas, and climbing into her car. She was out on the main highway before the reality of what had happened fully hit. She fist-pumped and screamed for at least a couple miles before pulling over to the side of the road and breaking into tears.

Finally, *finally*, something had gone right. Once she started at the Richardson Ranch, she'd be fully employed. She wouldn't have to give up her apartment, would have money to help her mother, money for a class every semester. Plus, she was working in a beautiful setting for an employer who seemed as perfect as his home.

Life couldn't get much better.

•••

"Are you sure about what you just did, Jack?" Anne asked.

"Even without considering the other applicants, she seems perfect," he replied.

"She's certainly not who I had in mind for taking care of the boys. She's young, for one thing."

"The others I interviewed were younger. You weren't here for the high-school-aged girls who interviewed with me earlier in the week. You only got to see Quanna and one other person."

"All right. I'll give you that. But this one has never taken care of kids before. And I doubt she's ever taken care of a place as nice as this one."

"From where I was sitting, she did just fine with Daniel and Lucas. And I'm not worried about her ability to do a little cleaning and cooking. Her references are impeccable. Look, Anne, I know you're protective of the boys, and I know you want only the best for them. But it's my call. And I think she's perfect. So does my Aunt Joan, if this morning's phone call is any indication."

"I guess that's about as good a recommendation as any. Still..."

He put his arm around her shoulder and hugged her. "I appreciate your concern, and I know how much you'll miss being with the boys every day. Really I do. But I'm confident she'll be fine. Stop worrying."

"Who'll be fine, Dad? What's Gramma worried about?" Daniel, who had apparently overheard the last part of the conversation, seemed concerned.

His son was a worrier. Jack knew he had to nip this in the bud. "She's not worried about anything, buddy. We're talking about how we're going to make the switch from her being here to Quanna taking over."

"Why can't we have Aunt Barbara or someone we know babysit us?" Daniel sought the solace of a hug from his grandmother who happily gave it to him.

"We've been over this already. Aunt Barbara has other responsibilities, and Gramma will be having surgery soon and will be out of commission. Aunt Joan says Quanna is perfect for this job, and I trust her judgment."

"But, Dad..."

"No buts, Daniel. It's done. Starting in a week, Quanna will be working here. And I expect you to treat her with the same respect you give your grandmother."

Daniel didn't look convinced. But, then, neither did Anne.

Chapter 3

Quanna's parents hadn't been able to afford the Barbie Dream House she'd wanted when she was a kid. But working at the Richardson Ranch was more than making up for her childhood disappointment. Barbie would eat her heart out if she saw this house. The kitchen was a pleasure to cook in, and the light housekeeping chores were hardly chores at all when they were done in such a pleasant setting.

Her daily tasks mainly consisted of keeping the kitchen clean, the boys' rooms and living areas tidied, and the laundry washed and put away. Apparently Jack and the boys did the rest of the cleaning on the weekends. Someone did—the place was always neat, and there was never any dust or dirt to be seen. Quanna did a few extra things to help, like wiping up the dirt tracked in by someone who forgot to remove his shoes, but mostly, she stuck to taking care of the kids and their belongings unless she was asked to do something else.

It had been awkward working with Anne Salazar for a week. She seemed distant, cool even. It was obvious she couldn't do many of the things that needed to be done, but it was also clear she wasn't crazy about the idea of handing it all over to someone else. Quanna wrote it off to the pain she was experiencing from her bad hip. At least, that's what she hoped it was and not something like being unhappy that Quanna was taking her job.

It was a relief when she was finally in charge of the job by herself. Trying to help the boys become comfortable with her, she changed little at first. There would be plenty of time later for new foods and routines. She figured out who ate which cereal and what their favorite lunch treats were and made sure to include what they liked in their meals. She asked them to help her set up a routine for doing homework and chores. Her own daily tasks were done while they were in school. Before she left each day, she prepared their evening meal and had the table set. The boys did the cleanup so well there was never a trace of a dirty dish or pan the next morning when she arrived.

But, although the boys did all their chores and homework as asked, nothing seemed to fully open up the lines of communication with her. They were never rude or mean. She assumed they'd been told to treat her politely and with respect because they did as she asked and never talked back. But they kept their distance, especially Daniel who only seemed to talk to her when she addressed him directly. Lucas was a bit more open, and she tried to cultivate him in hopes he would influence his brother.

She knew from overhearing some of their conversations they weren't crazy about having a stranger in place of their beloved grandmother, but she wasn't sure how to make it better. It was like being in charge of ghost kids, they were around her so infrequently, and when they were, they were quiet.

Their father was another matter. His presence was only too apparent. Not that he hovered. However, Quanna saw a lot more of him than she'd expected. He ran the ranch from his home office on the second floor. Most of the time, he was out in the barn or the fields, but some mornings and the occasional afternoon, he was in the house handling paperwork, making phone calls, and doing who-knew-what-else to keep the ranch going.

Then there was the outdoorsy, sage-y smell she was learning to associate with him. When she took towels from the master bathroom to fill a load of wash one day, she discovered it was from the soap he used. The scent lingered in her nostrils for the rest of the day, as did the image of him using the soap in the shower, making her think of him more than she should and in highly unprofessional ways.

His laundry sometimes made her blush when she folded it. Well, his black boxer briefs did. Not from touching the underwear itself but from the occasional thought that popped into her head of what he would look like wearing only what she was holding in her hands.

Unlike at the Golden Years where she had often joined the other women on staff in trying to catch a glimpse of him, in this job, she did what she could to stay out of his way. It was partly because she didn't want to be a nuisance, but she also had to admit she didn't want to deal with the attraction she felt when she was around him. After only a few weeks, she began to wonder if taking a job where she was in such close contact with someone who affected her so strongly had been such a good idea. She'd never had this kind of response to a man before. Her one serious relationship in Portland hadn't affected her the way Jack did. Most of the guys she'd dated had been more friends than anything else.

Almost every day, she started the morning reminding herself how important the job was to her. It would be stupid to mess it up by flirting with the boss. She'd be right back worrying about money again if it all blew up in her face. Besides, no matter how polite he was, it was certainly possible a woman who was half Indian, half Latina wasn't the kind of woman he was attracted to. Not to mention the kind of woman his friends would approve of for him. So she focused on making sure he was happy with her work and tried to ignore the growing attraction she felt for the man who signed her paycheck.

But managing her feelings about Jack was a minor challenge compared to the one she had trying to get her charges to warm up to her. After a few weeks, Lucas began to thaw. He was a naturally talkative and cuddly kid, and she was only too glad to engage in whatever conversation he wanted to have, as well as give him the hugs and cuddles he liked.

Daniel was another story. Her relationship with him improved so slowly she was sure she would never crack what seemed to be his determination to keep her at bay. She said nothing to Jack, always telling him things were great and hoping it would be true soon.

Then two incidents with the family's horses occurred.

The first happened when Jack invited her to join them on their weekly horseback ride. She was delighted to be asked and happy to say yes. On the specified day, she arrived at work wearing boots instead of her usual athletic shoes. Daniel immediately noticed.

"How come you're wearing boots?" he asked.

"Don't you remember? Your dad invited me to ride with you after school."

"Oh. I forgot."

He seemed more distant than usual, but Quanna forgot about it after the boys went off to school and she got caught up in her daily routine.

When Jack brought the boys home that afternoon, he suggested they eat their snack quickly and then go to the barn where Quanna knew there were four Appaloosa horses and a colt stabled: Jack's horse, Hero, Lucas's Spot, Daniel's Paint, and a fourth horse called Rose who had recently given birth to the colt Petal.

Quanna was tidying up the boys' books and jackets in the entryway when she heard Jack say, "Okay, guys, let's get going before we run out of daylight. Daniel, if you help Lucas saddle Spot, I'll saddle Hero and help Quanna get Rose ready."

"No. Quanna can't ride Rose," Daniel protested. "Rose isn't hers."

"I know she isn't, son," Jack said. He sounded patient as he explained. "But Rose is an easy horse to ride, and since I don't know how well Quanna rides, I thought..."

"You can't let her, Dad. It's not right." He sounded close to tears. "Rose doesn't belong to her."

"Okay, then you ride Rose and Quanna can ride Paint," Jack said.

"Rose isn't my horse either. I want to ride my horse." Daniel's voice was beginning to reach a pitch high enough to hurt human ears. "You can't let someone ride someone else's horse."

Quanna hurried to the kitchen, hoping to get there before Daniel burst into tears. "Jack, I've been thinking. As much as I appreciate your offer to let me ride with you, I better stay here. I haven't finished the laundry, and I haven't even started dinner yet. If it's okay with you, I'll take a rain check."

Jack's look of relief was all the signal she needed to know she'd made the right decision, although she had no idea why Daniel was so upset over which horse she rode.

"If that's what you think is best, that's what we'll do." He shooed the boys out the back door. "Let's get going, then." Before he followed them, he turned and mouthed the words, "Thank you."

Dismayed at Daniel's vehement objection to her riding with them, Quanna sought comfort in the routine of her job. She put the dishes and glasses from the afternoon snack into the dishwasher and began prepping dinner. When she was finished, she mixed up a batch of chocolate chip cookie dough and began to bake cookies. She hoped the process—and the smells—of baking would help her feel less hurt that Daniel seemed to be having so much trouble accepting her role in the household.

About an hour later, she heard the sound of horses on the gravel drive and saw the three Richardsons ride toward the barn. After they unsaddled and stabled their mounts, the two boys came into the kitchen through the mudroom. Lucas took off his boots and immediately raced into the family room. Daniel lingered in the kitchen, his eyes downcast, a stubborn expression on his face.

Finally he said, "I'm sorry I messed up the ride for you."

"I'm sorry something upset you. Do we need to talk about what it was? Did I do something?"

"You didn't do anything. And Dad already talked to me."

"Okay, as long as there's not a problem between us."

"There isn't." He began to edge toward the door to the living room, seeming to be anxious to escape. "I'm going upstairs."

"I made some cookies." She indicated the two cooling racks on the island breakfast bar. "Take one with you, if you like. I think I can convince your dad it's okay to have one before dinner."

Daniel grabbed a cookie and ran. He had been gone less than five minutes when Jack came in the house. He seemed almost as uncomfortable as his son had been. "Did Daniel apologize to you for screwing up your chance to ride with us?" he asked.

"He did, but he didn't explain. What was it all about?"

Jack sighed and ran his fingers through his hair, a gesture Quanna was beginning to recognize as a sign he was uncomfortable. "Rose was Paula—his mother's—horse. I thought he'd be okay with your riding her, but he wasn't. He wouldn't even ride her himself. I didn't check with him beforehand, and I should have. He was hit particularly hard by Paula's death. Didn't—wouldn't—talk about it for months. We all went to a counselor, and it helped some. Lately, he's been talking about her a little more. I thought ... well, I guess I was too hopeful."

"It isn't hard to understand how he feels. I know how hard it was for me when my dad died a few years ago, and I was a lot older than Daniel."

"Still, he wasn't thinking about your feelings, which is what he should have apologized for."

"He did fine. Don't worry about it." She pointed to the cooling racks. "I made his favorite cookies. Maybe that'll get me a few points with him. I also told him I'd convince you it was okay that he took one upstairs with him."

"Ordinarily, I'd say 'you lose,' but I'll let it slide this time. Thank you for understanding." He grinned at her as he grabbed a handful of cookies. "And for letting me take more than one of these before dinner."

She watched him saunter into the living room and wondered if she had ever known anyone who could make the sun come out with just a grin the way Jack Richardson could.

Chapter 4

Oddly enough, the incident over the horseback ride seemed to help Quanna's relationship with Daniel. At least, he began to have conversations with her instead of merely answering the questions she asked of him. He even let her give him a slight hug when she sent him off to school. Sometimes. It wasn't the warmer relationship she was beginning to have with his brother, but it was better than it had been.

Then the second incident involving the family's Appaloosas occurred.

This one started when Daniel walked in from school and said, "Where's Dad? It's our day to go riding." He obviously knew, from the absence of the family pickup in the drive, his father wasn't home. His scrunched up face and tone of voice showed his displeasure.

"I don't know. He's been gone all day," Quanna answered. "But I wouldn't worry if I were you. He always makes good on his promises. Why don't you take your snack into the dining room and get started on your homework while you wait for him?"

When the look on his face didn't change, it was obvious her response hadn't been the one he wanted. He muttered something unintelligible as he slung his backpack onto the bench in the entry, took out two books and a notebook, and strode off to the kitchen without saying anything more. Lucas, who was smart enough to stay out of the line of fire when his older brother was in a bad mood, grabbed his books and followed, also without a word.

"I was about to go upstairs to finish the laundry," Quanna called after them. "But if you need help with your homework, I can stay downstairs."

She got the answer she expected, given the look on Daniel's face—no response. *Oh, well. Two steps forward, one step back.* Mentally shrugging her shoulders, Quanna went upstairs.

Perhaps it was the sting of the dismissal. Or she could have been preoccupied with the chore she was trying to finish. The noise of the dryer might have obscured what was going on downstairs. Or more accurately, what *wasn't* going on. Whatever the reason, somehow she didn't pick up on the lack of noise. If she'd been aware of the silence, she'd have known something was up. The two boys were always talking to each other when they thought adults were out of earshot, even if it was only to bicker about who should get the bigger cookie. Chatterbox Lucas made sure of that.

When she went downstairs twenty minutes later to check on her charges, she not only heard how quiet it was but she discovered why—the boys were nowhere to be found. They were not in the dining room, although their books were. They weren't in the kitchen, although the empty plates from the apple slices and crackers spread with peanut butter she'd prepared for them were in the sink.

Calling their names, she checked the family room but found no evidence they'd been there. She went back upstairs, thinking they may have slipped past her to their rooms while she was occupied with laundry. But their rooms were as empty of their presence as the rest of the house was.

Panicked, she ran down the steps and out the back door, hoping they'd gone to the barn to do their chores. Before she could get halfway to her goal, Daniel rode up on his horse.

"Daniel, what are you doing? You know your dad doesn't want you riding without an adult with you." She grabbed at the bridle of the horse to stop him. "You were supposed to wait for him to come home and go with you."

"He was taking too long. I wanted to go for a ride before it got dark so we went on our own."

She was about to lay into him for disobeying when she noticed his face, which looked like every drop of blood had been drained from it. And she realized what—or who—wasn't with him. "Where's your brother?"

He hitched his chin in the direction from which he'd come. "Back there. Spot must have stumbled or something and threw Lucas. He landed funny. He might have ... maybe he broke his arm. I tried to get him to ride back here, but he wouldn't get back on Spot. He says it's because his arm and leg hurt. But I think it's because he's afraid."

Two emotions hit Quanna at the same time—concern for Lucas and anger at Daniel for disobeying, knowing as surely as she knew her own name Lucas hadn't come up with the idea of riding on his own. A third emotion—fear of what Jack would say—tried to elbow its way into her consciousness, but she wouldn't let it. She had other things to deal with.

"Stay here. Do not move. And I mean it. Not an inch. I need to find something I can use for a splint. Then you're going to take me to him." She found small boards and several old, clean towels that were used to wipe down the horses after a ride and returned. "I'm going to ride behind you. Take your foot out of the left stirrup and hold Paint still."

Daniel didn't argue or hesitate, but did as she demanded. When she'd mounted the horse and settled into the saddle behind him, he said, "You did that like you've ridden a lot."

"We can talk about my riding experiences later. I need to get to Lucas. Take me to him."

In less than five minutes, they came upon a small ball of little boy, huddled on the ground, Spot's reins in his left hand. Lucas's face was dusty and tear-streaked. From the abnormal angle of his right arm, Quanna was sure at least one of the bones in his forearm was broken.

When she dismounted and ran to him, her splint materials in hand, he struggled to stand up but seemed to have difficulty with his right leg. "Did you hurt your leg, too?" she asked.

"I think I sprained my ankle," he said. And burst into fresh tears.

She held the sobbing boy in her arms for a few moments then sat down with him in her lap and began to carefully probe his arm. She was relieved to find that the broken bone had not pierced the skin, and he had a strong pulse in his wrist. After explaining how she was going to make his arm more comfortable for the ride home, she put her words into action, tearing the towels into strips and securing the two boards with them.

Daniel stood nearby, holding the reins of the two horses, silent, pale, and big-eyed.

When she'd finished applying the splint, she carefully lifted Lucas so he could put his left foot in the stirrup, and he mounted Spot. Quanna rode behind him. When they reached the ranch house, she told Daniel to take the horses to the barn while she wrapped Lucas's ankle and made two phone calls. She made the easy one—to the family's pediatrician—first. Then, after a deep breath and with shaking hands, she let Jack know his son had broken his arm and she was about to take him to the emergency room.

Jack seemed calm on the phone, insisting she wait for him. He was only five minutes out. He would take Lucas to the ER. But she knew by the speed with which his truck roared down the road and the way gravel sprayed as he slammed on the brakes, it wasn't going to be a cool and reasoned conversation when he got in the house.

She was right.

The two boys and Quanna were sitting at the breakfast bar in the kitchen when he strode into the room. Daniel was nibbling on cookies she'd given him to comfort him. Quanna was rubbing Lucas's back as he sniffed back tears and pushed around a few cookie crumbs.

"What the hell happened here?" Jack demanded as he inspected his son's splinted arm.

"The boys went horseback riding and..."

"They're not allowed to go out without an adult with them. They knew I would be here. I was less than five minutes away when you called."

"I know, but..."

"You know? But you let them go alone?" Jack's voice got louder with each sentence. "They're too young to be riding unsupervised. You were told to have them wait for me. That was your job today. A job, I'll remind you, I pay you for."

Quanna guessed from the tight-lipped, frightened expression on Daniel's face he wasn't going to confess to being the instigator of the ill-fated ride. She didn't blame him, actually, for not owning up to it. Jack Richardson on a tear was intimidating.

"I'm disappointed in you, Quanna. I expected more from someone who came with such good recommendations. But what I apparently got was someone who doesn't pay attention to what my kids do and lets them run wild." He was pacing the kitchen floor now, his anger growing with each step. "And why are you feeding him? If they have to operate, he needs an empty stomach."

"I called his pediatrician, and she said it was okay to give him something if he wanted it. She'll x-ray his arm to make sure, but from what I described, she thinks it's a simple fracture. He'll only need a cast. Even if he does need surgery, she said it wouldn't be today. It would have to be after the swelling goes down. She's on her way to the ER now. I would have driven him there but..."

"I'll take care of my sons myself, thank you." Jack had stopped his pacing and was standing in front of Lucas. "Come on, buddy, let's get you to the doctor."

Lucas hopped down from the stool and almost crumpled on the floor.

"You hurt your leg, too?"

Lucas nodded, tears beginning again.

Quanna said, "It's his right ankle. I wrapped it. I don't think it's broken."

"I'd prefer to have the doctor make the diagnosis." Jack picked up his younger son and headed for the door. "Daniel, come with me. You're not staying here alone. Quanna's leaving."

"Yes, Dad." Daniel gave a quick look at Quanna and followed his father to his truck.

Quanna cleaned up the milk-and-cookie dishes and locked up the house. She was about to drive off when she remembered Spot and Paint. They hadn't been taken care of after their aborted expedition. She unsaddled the horses, wiped them down, fed and watered them, and put them in their stalls. At least she wouldn't be blamed for something happening to valuable animals. Just valuable children.

Getting back into her car, she wondered if that would be the last thing she ever did for the Richardson family. She needed a shoulder to cry on and maybe a good meal. She called her friend Rita and asked her to meet her at the Cowboy Up Bar and Grill.

• • •

Jack had a phone call to make, an apology to get off his chest, and a couple of upset kids to deal with. There was also a meeting this evening of the wheat co-op he ran to discuss the summer's harvest schedule. It was the last thing he needed, but unfortunately, it had taken a couple weeks to find a date and time when everyone could get together, which meant there was no way to get out of it. So, after Lucas had his arm and his ankle x-rayed, the first limb casted, and the second one wrapped, Jack dropped the boys off at his sister's then raced back to Pendleton. He made it to the restaurant where his fellow co-op members were meeting for dinner only a little later than he was expected.

But as he strode through the bar to the restaurant in back where they always met, he noticed two young men in jeans and Western shirts around the high bar table of a woman he could only see from the back, perched on a stool. From what he could see, she had a nice figure. She wore her long, dark hair in a loose, low ponytail that swished back and forth as she looked from one man to the other. Both the men appeared to be drunk and, from their body language, trying to intimidate her. He knew the type. Not only were they full of booze, they were full of themselves and out to make trouble. The woman, he decided, could use a little help. So he changed directions. As he approached the table, he heard some of the conversation, which confirmed his suspicions.

"Come on, honey. You know you want it. You all want to be with a white guy."

"What I want," the woman responded, her voice soft but unwavering, "is for you to leave me alone."

"No you don't. You're jush playing hard to get," the second man said, his slurred words showing just how drunk he was. "We'll show you a good time, I promish."

"Please. Leave. Or I'll call the manager."

"No one caresh what happens to shum Indian tramp," the first man said, grabbing at her.

She evaded his hand. "Don't touch me, or I'll do more than call the manager. I'll call the cops." She took a phone out of her purse, a vaguely familiar looking purse, although Jack didn't know why.

"I believe the lady asked you to leave. Do it," he said, walking up to the table.

When the woman turned around, Jack realized why the purse was familiar. It belonged to Quanna. A Quanna who looked quite different sitting in his favorite restaurant with her hair loose and a little bit of lipstick on.

The second drunk said, "Go away, old man. Thish is none of your business."

"I'm making it my business. Leave as you were asked to do, or I'll get the restaurant manager. He'll be glad to help you out, although you might not like his methods. And, since his brother the sheriff is on speed dial, I imagine he'll be asking for assistance from him, too."

"Fuck off." The more aggressive of the two fended off the attempts of his friend to get him to leave. "I'm not scared of you."

Jack shrugged. "Your call." He turned and waved toward the back. "Ray," he yelled. "Want to come out here and help me get rid of a couple drunks?"

The manager, a tall, muscular man who looked like he could bench-press twice his weight came from the back of the restaurant, a cell phone at his ear.

The two young men took one look at what was headed toward them and made tracks for the door. Jack waved off Ray who gave him a thumbs-up.

"You okay?" he asked Quanna.

"Yes. Thanks."

She didn't make eye contact when she spoke. He wasn't sure if it was because she was angry, embarrassed, or insulted. Maybe all three. "I'm sure you could have handled it on your own. But a little backup is never a bad thing, is it?"

"I suppose it isn't." She was playing with the napkin under the full glass of wine in front of her, tearing off small pieces of it as if it were more important than looking directly at him.

"Actually, I'm glad I ran into you. Do you mind if I sit down for a minute? I have something I need to say to you."

She sighed, waved at the bar stool across from her, and said, "Sure. Might as well get it over with tonight and not wait for tomorrow."

"I'm not sure I'd put it that way, but thanks." He took a seat and waited, hoping she'd stop reducing the napkin to pulp and meet his eyes. When she didn't, he began, "I owe you an apology. A big one."

That got her attention. "Wait. What? An apology? Why?"

"For the way I talked to you this afternoon. I shouldn't have said most of what I did. Any of what I said, actually. My only explanation is I was scared. Nothing like that has ever happened to one of the boys, and it scared the pea-wadding green out of me. But it's not an excuse for my taking it out on you."

She was silent, her eyes wide and her lips parted, as if trying to say something that wouldn't come out. "It's ... it's okay. I understand. I was scared, too."

"I guess we all were. Particularly Daniel, as it turns out. Which is why he didn't say anything about his role in the whole thing until we'd been to the doctor and were on the way to my sister's house. Then he confessed he was the instigator. He'd waited until you were busy so you wouldn't notice they weren't in the house. He was pissed at me for not being there after school so he talked Lucas into going out on their own."

"I figured it was something like that."

"But you didn't confront him when I was yelling at you for something you didn't do."

"I wanted him to tell you on his own, not because I backed him into a corner. And I might have felt a little guilty about not knowing what they were up to."

"They're not toddlers. I didn't hire you to stalk them."

Before she could say any more, Doreen, one of the members of the wheat co-op, approached the table. She was well dressed, as always. "There you are, Jack. The crew sent me out to see if your truck was around anyplace so we knew whether to expect you any time soon." She put her hand on Jack's shoulder in a familiar way. She'd been doing things like that for some time no matter how he tried to discourage it. "We can't start without you, can we?" She was staring at Quanna as she spoke.

"I'll be there in a minute or two, Doreen." He motioned from one woman to the other. "This is Quanna Morales, my kid wrangler. Quanna, this is Doreen Campbell. She runs the Lazy C."

"Oh, what a sweet title for a nanny! You're so clever, Jack." Doreen put out her hand to Quanna, and the two women briefly shook, although Doreen quickly returned her attention to Jack. "I'll tell them to expect you soon. So don't spend too much time out here. After all, you can see your nanny when she comes to work for you."

"I'll be right there." He waited until she was out of earshot before saying, "Now, where was I?"

"You better get to your meeting, hadn't you?" Quanna said.

"Not until I'm sure you accept my apology and I know we're okay."

"Of course I accept your apology."

"And we're all right? If I screwed up and you quit, the boys would be disappointed. They like your cooking better than their grandmother's. And even Daniel was beginning to think you were better at what you do than she was. But you sealed the deal with them today. In the car on the way to the doctor, they told me how amazing you were about Lucas's arm. They're impressed with your first aid skills. Daniel is grateful you didn't dime him out, and they both think you're a better rider than I am. If that's possible." He smiled, hoping he could get her to do the same.

"This was not the way I hoped to impress them."

"You and me both. But it's how it happened. So, are we okay?"

"We're fine, Jack. Really."

"Good. Then I'll see you in the morning at the usual time." He got up from the table and had taken only a few steps toward the back when he heard her say, "Crap."

She was looking at her phone and frowning.

"Problem?"

"The friend who was supposed to meet me just canceled." She rummaged around in her purse, came up with a handful of dollar bills, and threw them on the table. "I might as well go home. I hate to eat alone in a restaurant."

"I'll walk you to your car."

"I'll be fine. You get to your meeting."

"Those two drunks might be outside waiting for you. You shouldn't go out there alone. I'll walk you to your car."

When she stood, he noticed, for the first time, how the jeans she wore hugged every curve she had. He also noticed she had an interesting set of them. There was something about her tonight that made him look at her quite differently than he did at the ranch. Maybe it was the lighting in the bar.

As they got to the door of the restaurant, Jack reached in front of her to open it, placing his hand on the small of her back as he did. He felt something when he touched her, a slight shock, like he'd walked across a rug and picked up an electric charge, although the floor in the bar was smooth, glossy wood. What the hell? And had she felt it, too?

He dropped his hand as soon as she got through the door, and they walked silently to her car. She unlocked it, and he opened the door for her.

"Thank you," she said. "But I don't think it was necessary."

"You're wrong. Those two jerks are standing across the street staring at us," Jack said. "Get in the car and lock the doors. I'll wait until I'm sure they don't try to follow you home."

He watched her until her car was out of sight before he headed back to the restaurant.

He tried not to think about what had happened when he touched her. But he couldn't. Tonight he'd seen her for the first time as a beautiful woman, not just the pretty girl who took care of his kids. Images of her silky black hair free and falling over coppery brown skin flashed through his mind. Skin that would be soft and smooth to the touch. His touch. While they were both in his bed.

Wait. Why the hell was he was thinking about her hair or the feel of her skin? He hadn't thought about a woman in that way for so long he had pretty much assumed the possibility was, sadly, all in his past or so far in his future as to be virtually unattainable. This was a hell of an inconvenient time for the reemergence of his heretofore-slumbering libido, not to mention an inappropriate person to have awakened it. Besides, he was way too old for her. Or she was too young for him. Either way, thinking about hitting on a person who worked for him was not only out of character but too cliché to consider.

He put any thought of acting on his impulses out of his head and went into a meeting about harvest schedules and grain prices. Things he knew more about than he did what to do about being unexpectedly attracted to the kid wrangler he saw every day in every room of his house.

Chapter 5

When Quanna let herself into the house the next morning, it was quieter than usual. She wasn't sure whether it meant things were going smoothly in spite of the drama of the night before or if it was the calm before another storm. She'd been there about half an hour, making coffee and getting breakfast ready, before anyone appeared.

Daniel came downstairs first.

"Dad says I owe you another apology."

"Did he?"

"I got you in trouble by not owning up to what I'd done. But I told him last night on the way to Aunt Barb's. Honest I did. I don't think he's mad at you anymore."

"He isn't. We ran into each other last night after you went to the doctor's, and he told me about your conversation. We're fine." She handed the cereal bowls to him. "Why don't you put these out on the dining room table? I'll bring the placemats. I think Lucas will be more comfortable eating out there with his cast and his ankle."

"First ... uh ... I'm sorry. You shouldn't have gotten yelled at for something I did."

"I accept your apology. Now, let's get breakfast going before your carpool gets here." She was in the doorway of the dining room when she felt, rather than saw, Jack in the kitchen. From the sounds, he was pouring himself a cup of coffee.

"I'm driving them to school today, Quanna. I want to talk to Lucas's teacher about how we're going to manage this." He paused for a moment. "Can I get you some coffee?"

Without turning, she said, "Yes, thanks, that would be great."

"Black, one sugar, right?"

She was so surprised he'd noticed how she took her coffee she almost didn't respond. "Ah, right. Thanks." She handed the placemats to Daniel to continue setting the table and returned to the kitchen.

"Here you go," Jack said and handed her coffee in the mug she usually used. He knew her favorite. Another surprise. His fingers brushed hers as she took the cup, and the same frisson of electricity she'd felt when he'd touched her the night before startled her fingers. She had to concentrate not to drop the mug. When she looked up, she saw his eyes had darkened and knew he'd felt it, too.

Fortunately, the patient came limping into the room, demanding attention with sighs and a pathetic "good morning."

"Wow. A bright blue cast. How cool is that," Quanna said. "You'll be the hit of your class."

The attempt at being pathetic disappeared in a grin and a wave of the affected arm. "I got to pick the color. It's made of glass ... something."

"Fiberglass," Jack and Quanna said in unison, quickly glancing at each other, then just as quickly looking away. Quanna was sure she was blushing.

Lucas didn't seem to notice. "The doctor had five colors to pick from. Do we have a Sharpie I can take to school so my friends can sign it?"

Grateful for the excuse to get away from the sudden heat that seemed to be shimmering between her and her boss, Quanna rummaged through the junk drawer in the breakfast bar and came up with the requested Sharpie.

"How about you start on your breakfast before you plan out the autographs on your cast?" Jack said. "I'll take out the cereal if you'll get the milk and juice, Quanna."

"Who's gonna help me pour stuff?" Lucas asked, the pathetic tone reappearing. "I can't use my right hand."

"I'll help until you get used to using your left hand," Jack answered.

And with that, the morning routine kicked in and the atmosphere lightened. For the moment.

•••

Within a week, the new normal for the family was as familiar as the old normal had once been. Lucas seemed to revel in his popularity at school, which had already been high because he was such a congenial kid but was now over the top thanks to his tale of horseback adventure and the resulting blue cast. He also undoubtedly enjoyed the attention he was getting from his father and brother, the latter mostly out of guilt for being the cause of his injury.

He coerced Quanna into being his homework scribe after school. He solved the problems and did the thinking; she did the writing. He still complained about homework, especially math, even with her help. His "theory" was it was stupid to learn something a computer could do for you. In an attempt to get him to see the usefulness of what he was complaining about, Quanna finally asked one day, "What are you interested in, if not math and science?"

"The Roman gods and goddesses," Lucas said. "Or Egyptology. I think I'll study ancient Egypt when I grow up."

"Yeah, because studying dead Egyptians is such a useful thing to do," his brother, who had finished his homework without complaint, muttered.

Quanna was afraid the conversation was headed for a rare quarrel so she intervened quickly. "Archaeologists use math and science in their work. If you want to be one, you have to learn the tools they use."

"I'll hire someone to do the math. I'll do the research." Lucas dismissed the argument with a wave of his casted hand.

Sighing, Quanna said, "I give up. Your dad can help with the rest of your math after dinner, which I better get to preparing. Then I should get home and finish the reading for my class."

"But we haven't worked on my essay for Ms. Eagleman yet," Lucas said. "And the sloppy copy's due tomorrow."

"You can work on it after dinner," Jack said as he joined them. "We can't keep Quanna here all evening because you've been putting off writing it by complaining about your math homework."

"But Quanna's good at essays, Dad." He turned his big brown eyes to Quanna and begged. "Please, please, please stay for dinner and help me with my essay. Please."

Jack said, "You're welcome to stay, Quanna. But I don't want you to think you have to because Lucas is begging."

"I don't want to intrude on family time." She tried to sound firm in her refusal even though the thought of eating dinner with Jack was more attractive than it should be. To Lucas, she said, "Your dad can help you with the essay, can't he?"

"No. It's about him," Lucas said. "Can't you stay this once? Please?"

"That's five pleases," Jack said. "Some kind of record." His smile was more inviting than any number of pleases.

"I guess I'm staying then," Quanna said.

Sitting at the table with the three Richardson males, catching Jack's eye when one of the boys said something funny, earning a grin from him when she said something he liked, was both fun and a challenge. On one hand, she loved the attention he was paying her, which felt more personal than professional. On the other, she had to keep her feelings at bay while still engaging as the boys' "kid wrangler."

The other challenge was to keep from getting caught in the warmth of being part of a family, especially this family, with a man she found so attractive and kids she had learned to love. She barely tasted the food she ate trying to keep her conflicting emotions in balance.

After dinner, Lucas was excused from dish duty while Quanna helped him craft the first draft of his essay. It was a relief to have Jack in the kitchen during this process, as Lucas's assignment was to write about someone who had been important in his life. As Lucas had said, he'd chosen his dad, which wasn't great for Quanna's peace of mind.

The exercise began with a laundry list of Jack Richardson's virtues. And as Quanna already knew, he had many, although it was tempting to add a few to Lucas's list. Not only was he a great dad who looked after his boys with care and love, as Lucas pointed out, but his protective streak extended to women alone in bars. And he was the fantasy hero of half the staff of the Golden Years Retirement Center. But that probably wasn't an appropriate addition to his son's essay, although it was pretty high on Quanna's list of his virtues.

• • •

Jack stayed in the kitchen after he and Daniel loaded the dishwasher. He told his son it was to finish wiping up the counters and set up the coffeepot for the morning. It was actually so he could eavesdrop on the conversation in the dining room. He told himself he was curious about what his son was writing about him, but he knew he really wanted to hear what Quanna would say.

What he heard made the eavesdropping well worth it. Lucas talked about what a great dad he had, and Quanna agreed that he had an "amazing father." As an additional highlight, Luke made a couple jokes and she laughed, giving Jack the chance to hear the musical sound of her laugh, which he'd grown to like. He listened as she gently prodded Lucas to get ideas from him and to organize them into something resembling an essay. Between his pleasure at what Lucas said and Quanna's reaction to it, his ego was stroked quite nicely before the hour was up and the draft Lucas needed for the next day was ready to turn in.

"I'll let your dad finish up your math with you," Quanna said. She picked up the textbooks and notebooks she'd piled on the sideboard. "Time for me to get home and do my own homework."

She was headed for the front door when Jack interrupted her departure. "Let me walk you out. I want to talk to you." He noticed she seemed to walk far ahead of him through the living room, perhaps in a hurry to get away.

He followed her to her car. The sweet smell of the plains mingled with the spicy smell he'd begun to associate with being around her. It was a combination hard to resist.

When they got to her car, he touched her arm to turn her toward him. "I don't think I've told you how much I appreciate what you've done helping Lucas since he broke his arm. Both the boys love having you around. So do I." He added quickly, "Appreciate having you here, I mean."

"I'm glad you're happy with my work."

He noticed she emphasized the words *my work*. "We're more than happy. All three of us. You've made a big difference in our lives."

She seemed nervous, dropping her gaze and jingling her car keys. "Thank you for saying such kind things."

"Not kind. The truth."

He shifted gears away from a subject that seemed to be embarrassing for her. "There's something else I wanted to talk to you about. I don't want the boys to get excited before I decide if it's going to work out, which is why I wanted to do this out here." He ran his hands through his hair. "Before the boys' mother was sick, my brother and I used to swap kids every summer. Sam, my brother, wants his boys to have some appreciation for the kind of life we lived growing up. After his boys were here for a couple weeks, I sent Daniel to the city. Luke would be old enough now to go, too."

There was an awkward pause as he tried to figure out how to say what he wanted to say. "The thing is, Sam called today and asked if I had thought about reinstating the tradition. It wasn't possible when Anne was taking care of the boys. She could never handle four of them. Not sure too many people would want to, actually."

"But you'd like me to," she finished for him. "I'd love it."

"You'd take on all four of them for two weeks?"

"If your nephews are anything like your sons, it won't be a problem."

"Actually, they're a bit older. Maybe a bit more civilized. And they wouldn't be with you all day. Usually in the summer, the boys help me all morning and aren't around the house until after lunch. So, if you're sure..."

"I am."

"Thank you. I'll call Sam and tell him it's a go. Of course your pay will increase the two weeks Sammy and Jack are here."

"Your brother named his sons for the two of you?"

"Yeah, gets a little complicated when we're all together, but it was an honor. Anyway, I'll increase your pay for those two weeks and give you vacation with pay the two weeks Lucas and Daniel are gone."

"That's way too generous, Jack. I can't take two whole weeks off and expect you to pay me."

"No, it's not. You'll earn it, believe me, with four boys here."

"How about I work half time while they're in Portland?"

"Two days a week with pay for all five. And I'll make sure you get overtime pay for tonight, too."

"Please, I don't want to be paid for tonight. I stayed because I wanted to. And staying here for dinner meant I didn't have to go home and cook." She put her hand up as if to ward off the money.

He captured it with both of his. It was a big mistake. He hadn't counted on his body's reaction to touching her. Completely inappropriate thoughts crowded his mind. Like what it would be like to touch her cheek or kiss her luscious pink lips. What her body would feel like pressed against his.

He felt the warmth of the hand he held and wanted to hold it for a good long time. He knew he needed to back off. He couldn't just drop her hand like a rock, though. So he made a clumsy attempt to turn their connection into a handshake. It didn't work.

Quanna tried to untangle their hands but that made it even more awkward, which seemed to embarrass her, if her slight blush was any indication. To cover his inept gesture, he continued the talk of salary. "We can negotiate pay later. Thanks for agreeing to the change in plans for the summer. You're invaluable around here."

"Thanks. Again." She withdrew her hand and opened her car door.

He watched her drive away, shaking his head after he was sure she couldn't see him anymore, wondering how the hell it had gotten so difficult to talk to an employee. A beautiful, smart, sexy, and totally entrancing employee.

Dear God, he was in over his head.

Chapter 6

After the essay-writing evening, at least once a week, one of the boys, usually Lucas, came up with a reason for Quanna to stay for dinner. As time went on, it became almost routine for her to be there once or twice a week. The issue of overtime pay got settled the way she wanted it: she had no intention of being paid for a social evening and a good meal.

There was no repeat of the hand-holding incident, for which Quanna was grateful. Sort of. She had loved the feel of his hand, loved the look in his eyes when he told her how much she was appreciated. It had become her favorite just-before-sleep thought. One that usually guaranteed lovely dreams. She knew she was embarking on the slipperiest of slopes, fantasizing about Jack, spending free time with the three of them, but she loved being around the three Richardsons so much she was willing to try to keep her balance.

With the arrival of summer came changes in Quanna's routine with the boys. First, they were around more every day, and she had to organize something to occupy their time when they weren't out helping their dad with ranch chores. Once a week, they went someplace the kids had not been to or wanted to visit again— the Tamastslikt Cultural Institute on the reservation, with its exhibits on the history of the American Indians who had lived in the area for centuries, was one. There were picnics, trips to the library, an occasional movie. They built raised beds in the garden and planted vegetables in them. She even started giving the boys cooking lessons.

Caught up in the busiest time of the year on his ranch, Jack wasn't around much except first thing in the morning and late in the afternoon, just before she left. Once a week or so, she had dinner with the family, reminding her of how strong the attraction to him was. A reminder she kept pushing out of her mind so she could focus on her job and the importance it had for both her and her family.

When the end of July arrived, so did Jack's nephews. Except for the increase in laundry and the huge amounts of food it took to keep four active boys from being hungry, they were easy to deal with. Each morning, they enthusiastically worked with Jack getting ready for harvest, and they often rode horses with their Aunt Barbara and her boys at Barbara's ranch where there were enough horses for everyone. They didn't mind mucking out the stables because, as they told Quanna, it made them feel like real cowboys. Even when Jack's other three nephews were in Quanna's charge, which happened a couple times during the visit, it was more pleasure than problem.

The two-week visit seemed to rush by. Before Quanna knew it, she was packing clothes for Daniel and Lucas's stay in Portland and then hugging all four boys goodbye before they piled into Jack's truck for a trip to the big city.

• • •

"For chrissake, Jack, light someplace, will you? I have a crick in my neck from trying to follow your pacing, and you're driving Chihuly nuts."

Jack dropped into the leather couch opposite the one his brother Sam was occupying. The two men looked so much alike they would have been hard pressed to deny their relationship. Jack had two inches and a few years on his younger sibling, but that was about all that was different.

Well, except for the expressions currently on their faces. Sam looked relaxed and content with himself. Jack was sure he projected neither quality.

Before he responded to his brother's complaint, Jack motioned for Chihuly, the curly-coated retriever Sam had acquired when he married Amanda St. Clair, to sit beside him. "Sorry. I guess I'm restless today." He scratched a spot between the dog's ears, hoping to make up for his pacing.

"No shit, Sherlock. It doesn't take my finely honed investigative skills to figure that out. What's going on?"

"Nothing I can't handle." Jack concentrated on the dog's head, avoiding his brother's eyes. "I'm not much of a city guy, I guess. I love your house, but I'm happier at the ranch."

"I get it, but this is more than wanting to be home in the wide open spaces of Umatilla County." Sam cocked his head and furrowed his brow. "It can't be money troubles. The last accountant's report on the ranch looked healthy. Is there something going on with the wheat crop this year?"

Jack shook his head, still not looking at his brother.

"Not money. Not wheat. Haven't heard of any cattle disease. And your boys are healthy and happy. That leaves woman troubles. You got something you want to talk about?"

Jack had never hid his personal life from his siblings, but he wasn't sure he wanted to be totally open with his brother right now. So he just kept scratching the dog's head and looking down. "Not really."

"Jack, I'm a cop. Every damn day of my life, I get lied to or have to put up with people trying to avoid telling me what I want to know. That's why we're given this bullshit meter when we graduate from the Academy. And right now, mine is pegged out at the high end of the scale. You might as well tell me so I don't have to resort to the thumbscrews we're also given along with our badges."

"There's nothing to tell. Nothing I want to tell, anyway."

"Who's this woman who finally got to you? Is it what's-her-name—Doreen—who's been running after ...? Wait, of course not. It's the pretty nanny, isn't it?"

Jack sighed and finally met his brother's gaze. "Leave it, Sam. I don't want to talk about it."

"Yeah, because stewing about it and wearing a rut in our wood floors is gonna solve the problem. Talking can't help."

"Jesus, what are we a couple of middle school girls? I can figure this out by myself."

"From where I'm sitting, you're not making much progress on that front. And, FYI, Chihuly needs the fur you're scratching off the top of his head."

"Shit. Sorry, boy." He discontinued his attention to the dog and stared at the ceiling for a few seconds. "How cliché can you get? The only woman who's interested me in God knows how long turns out to be my kids' nanny. Not only that, but she's so young, she could be my daughter. I've turned into a dirty old man."

"Oh, come on. Unless you hooked up with someone while you were dating Paula and have a daughter I don't know about, she couldn't be your daughter. Although if you did do something like that, Barb might know. I'll ask her."

"That's not what I meant and you know it. And for God's sake, don't bring our sister into this. If she ever found out..."

"If she found out you'd finally decided you're too young to be alone and started looking at an attractive woman the way a man should look at her, she'd be happy for you."

"Or ream me out."

"Come on, Jack. We all know Paula made you promise you wouldn't be alone after she was gone. When are you going to stop looking out for everyone else and start looking out for yourself? And why would you want to fly solo when you have a pretty woman who might want to fly with you?"

"Quanna's not merely pretty. She's beautiful. And smart and funny and warm and..." He shook his head at the smirk on his brother's face. "Leave it, Sam. She's too young. Not only that, but she works for me and has shown no interest in me as anything more than her employer."

"She doesn't seem too young to me. And from the way she looks at you when she thinks you're not paying attention, she's interested."

"You met her for all of, what, ten minutes when you brought the boys to the ranch. That makes you an expert, does it?"

"More like twenty-four hours and, again, I refer you to how I make a living. I know how to read people. She's interested. I'd bet my retirement on it."

"I notice you have nothing to say about her being my employee. An employee my kids love. The last thing I want to do is screw up the relationship she has with them."

"I agree it could be tricky. But thanks to me, you have two weeks without them to see if there's anything there." Sam leaned forward, his forearms on his thighs. "Seriously, Jack. I know you. You wouldn't say you were interested if this was only a passing fancy. Hell, you never asked another woman out after the first time you asked Paula for a date in eighth grade. You're a one-woman guy. Once someone catches your interest, that's it. If she's the one, you have to give it a chance to see if you can find something like I have with Amanda. Which, I'd remind you, occurred after a lot more complications than an age gap and an employment contract."

His brother had a point. Having the woman you love accused of murder so you had to help prove her innocence before you could tell her how you felt, as Sam had done, was considerably more difficult than anything he was dealing with.

"Maybe you're right. Maybe I should do something about it."

"Maybe your baby brother is right about what, Jack?" Amanda asked as she came into the living room. "You might as well tell me because he'll be bragging about it for weeks. He's so rarely in the driver's seat with his siblings."

Sam pulled his wife down onto the couch next to him. "Leave him alone, pretty lady. He's mulling over what to do about a woman."

"My two cents, for what it's worth, is that it's about time you did something about some woman, Jack. So stop mulling and start acting." She kissed her husband on the cheek. "Are you packed to go to the beach?"

"Yup. And so are our boys. I don't think Jack's boys even unpacked; they're so psyched to head for the ocean." He turned to his brother. "You coming to the coast with us?"

Jack didn't answer for a few moments. Then he slapped his hands on his knees and said, "You know what, I think I'll head back home today. No sense in driving to the beach only to turn around and drive home tomorrow."

"Right," Sam said. "It's the driving that decided it." He grinned before adding, "Good choice, brother. And good luck."

Chapter 7

During the four-hour drive from Portland to the Richardson Ranch, Jack had time to think about a lot of things. Like how he loved his brother and sister-in-law but didn't like urban life and didn't understand why Sam did. Like how much worse this visit had been than ones in the past because he not only missed the ranch, but he missed the woman he'd gotten used to seeing five days a week. Like how he didn't know what to do about wanting her to become more than merely the kid wrangler he paid to cook his meals and take care of his kids.

His kids. The only source of life in the house after Paula died wouldn't be there when he got home. He'd be alone for the first time since she'd gone. Not even Quanna would be there every day to keep him company. Would he be alone or lonely?

Quanna. He swore he could remember every conversation they'd had, every smile she directed at him, every joke of Lucas's she laughed at. It was hell that she was the only woman he'd met in years who attracted him. And doing anything about the attraction had the potential for being a complete disaster.

As he drove the last ten miles to the ranch, he concluded that maybe being in an empty house would give him the time to do what he'd told Sam he would do—figure it out. Maybe alone was the best thing to be at the moment.

Except when he opened the front door, he discovered that the house wasn't empty. He wasn't alone. Quanna was in the kitchen. She was at the sink, her back to the door from the living room, chopping something, onions he thought, and putting them into a bowl. She was singing. He listened for a few seconds, trying to identify the song but couldn't. Probably something someone his age wouldn't know.

He walked quietly toward the kitchen door, enjoying what he saw, not wanting her to know he was there quite yet. Dressed in a tank top and shorts, not her usual jeans and T-shirt, she had what seemed like miles of coppery skin on display. She was so damn beautiful it made his heart ache. In the months she'd been working for him, her open and loving ways with his sons had made her such an integral part of the family he didn't know what they would do if she left.

Which made his attraction to her dangerous. Not only was she young but she was too important to him, to his kids, to risk it all because he found her so alluring. His sons had already lost a mother to cancer and a grandmother to hip surgery. Thanks to Quanna, they were finally getting the stability they'd needed for a couple years. He couldn't risk screwing that up, no matter how attracted he was.

Besides, maybe she'd get pissed if he asked her out. Maybe she'd be repulsed. Okay, he knew that probably wasn't true. Even if he wasn't about to confess it to Sam, once or twice he thought he'd seen her look at him as more than her boss. Maybe more than once or twice, although it could have been his imagination. Or wishful thinking.

Either she sensed his presence or his jumbled thoughts had resulted in some noise emanating from him because without warning, she whirled around, the knife she was using pointed at him.

"Oh, God, Jack. You scared me." One hand held the knife; the other was covering her heart. Which, of course, drew his attention to her breast. Her nipple peeked through the thin cotton of her top, daring him to reach out, to touch.

He struggled to get his mind, and his eyes, off that tempting bit of flesh. "I'm sorry. I didn't mean to frighten you. I tried to make some noise when I came in so you'd know someone was in the house." It was a lie, but he didn't want her to know he'd been staring at her.

"Well, I didn't hear you."

"Would you mind putting the knife down? I'd rather continue the conversation without worrying you're about to use it on me." He smiled.

She looked down at her hand as if seeing it for the first time. "Aiming a weapon at your employer is probably not listed as acceptable behavior in the nanny handbook." She dropped the knife onto the kitchen island. "I'm sorry. But you did frighten me. I didn't think you were coming back until Monday."

"And I didn't think anyone would be here when I got home. What're you doing here on a Sunday? Didn't we agree before I left for Portland you had some down time coming? I thought you were only working Tuesday and Thursday this week."

"I wanted to finish up the laundry from last week and prep some meals so you wouldn't have to cook when you got home." She waved in the direction of the bowl she'd been dumping onions into. "I was working on potato salad."

"I'd have thought you had your fill of cooking for the Richardsons over the last two weeks."

She laughed. "Luckily, I'm used to cooking for boys—I have two brothers. I know how much it takes to keep them from being hungry. And doing this today means it'll be easier when I'm here again."

"You've worked your tail off the past two weeks. You've earned a few days off." He went to the refrigerator and opened it. "But as long as you're here, how about joining me in a beer or a glass of wine? At least I can offer you that."

"Thanks, but as soon as I finish this and clean up, I have to drive home."

Still staring into the refrigerator so he didn't have to see her reaction when he asked the question, he said, "Or I could pour you a glass of wine and you could stay for dinner with me. I bet there's enough for both of us in what you've stocked up for me."

"I don't want to impose. I'll finish up..."

"You're not imposing. I'd like the company. Your company," he hastened to add as he turned around. "Please?"

He was relieved to see a small smile. Even more relieved when she said, "When Lucas asks me to stay for dinner, there are usually four or five pleases."

"True, but I have more dignity than he does. Although if I have to, I can whine with the best eight-year-olds. I'd prefer it doesn't come to that, however."

She laughed again. "All right. I won't make you stoop to his level. I'll graciously accept your invitation for dinner." She joined him at the refrigerator. All the cold it generated couldn't keep him from feeling the heat of having her so close as she reached around him and grabbed a paper-wrapped package. He could smell the vanilla spice aroma he associated with her and could feel his body's response to her nearness. Which meant he had to move away quickly before it became obvious to her, too.

"If you're in the mood," she said, "I pulled these steaks from the freezer a while ago and they feel like they're defrosted. And there's the potato salad and tomatoes from the boys' garden."

"I'm always in the mood for steak. Especially when it's from my own cattle." He took the package from her. "Wine or beer?"

"A little wine please. I'm not much of a drinker."

"Yeah, I noticed at Cowboy Up you barely touched your glass."

"I've seen too many people get into trouble with it. It's not worth it."

He poured her a half glass of wine and handed it to her, trying not to notice the way she licked her upper lip after she took the first sip. He tried not to think about what she would taste like with a rich, red wine on her lips.

Dinner. Focus on dinner. "If you're about ready to eat, I'll take those steaks out to the grill."

"Perfect. I'll get the table set and the potato salad and tomatoes ready."

Grilling the steaks gave him time to collect his thoughts, to talk himself back from the edge of the cliff he'd impulsively walked out onto when he asked her to stay for dinner. It had been so long since he'd had dinner with a woman not related to him that he was as nervous as a teenager. Which, come to think of it, was the last time he'd asked a woman out for the first time. The realization made him even more edgy. Would Quanna consider this a date? Was it? He wasn't sure. If she did, how should he handle it? Had dating rules changed? What would a woman expect these days?

Oh, hell, date or no date, one rule hadn't changed, he was sure. He forgot to ask her how she liked her steak cooked.

He returned to the kitchen, the two steaks on a platter. "I hope you like medium rare. I forgot to ask. If you want it cooked some more..."

"No, medium rare is fine. Thanks." She grabbed another beer for him and her wine and headed for the dining room.

As they were about to sit down to dinner, Jack asked, "You probably would like some music, wouldn't you? You always seem to have some playing."

"That would be lovely."

He swapped the kids' iPod for his in the dock on the sideboard. The sound of classical music played softly as he settled himself at the table.

"I wouldn't have imagined you for a classical music fan," Quanna said as she dished up the salad.

"Not much choice in this house growing up. My mother was a classically trained pianist and taught all three of us—my brother, sister, and me. None of us had much talent for it. We did learn to love the music, however."

"I've wondered about the piano in the living room. Do you still play?"

There was a long pause before he answered. "Haven't for a while." There was another pause before he continued, not sure what the protocol was for discussing your late wife with the woman you'd invited to have dinner with you. "Actually, Paula was the one who played most often. She was one of the other kids my mother taught. Only one with any talent."

Both of them applied themselves to eating for a few minutes then Quanna asked, "Do you mind talking about Paula? I'd like to know more about her. The boys sometimes talk about her, and I've wondered. I mean, if it doesn't bother you."

"No, it doesn't bother me." He laid down his fork and knife and stared out into the room. "She was smart and talented. Loved music, obviously. Loved this part of the world. She never wanted to go anyplace on vacation because she was so happy being here."

"Lucas said she was a teacher."

"Yeah, kids were her greatest love. She taught first and second grade. There were dozens of her former students at her memorial service. Some of them were almost as broken up by her death as Daniel and Lucas were."

"Did you meet in college?"

"No, we grew up together. I asked her to a dance in, I think it was, the eighth grade and have never asked another girl out since then. We dated all through high school and went to Oregon State together. I never finished. But she got her degree, came home to teach, and we got married." He was quiet for a few long moments, continuing to look out into the room. Finally he said, "Was that what you wanted to know?"

"I didn't mean to upset you."

"You didn't. Not at all. I just realized I haven't talked about her with anyone outside the family in a long time."

Quanna said, "I've seen all the photos of her around the house. She was beautiful."

"She was a beautiful person. You'd have liked her. She would have liked you." He laughed. "Anyone who loves her kids the way you do would have been her friend forever." More silence.

"You must miss her."

"Haven't thought about that in a long time either. Guess I'd say, no, not the way I did at first. Sometimes when one of the kids does something special, I think how sad it is she isn't here to see it. But, as she kept saying when she was sick, life goes on." He shook his head. "Surely there must be something else we can talk about, isn't there?"

He could see the sympathy in her eyes and heard the soft tone in her voice when she said, "I'll change the subject, but thank you for sharing with me. I've wanted to ask, particularly because Daniel has begun to talk more about her, telling Lucas some of the things he remembers."

"I'm glad he is. Lucas worries about forgetting her. And, truth is, he was not quite six when she died, so he has foggy memories of her before she got sick to begin with. Daniel was older, and it's easier for him to remember. But he's been pretty closemouthed about her until recently."

"I actually think the Rose incident was healthy in a way, don't you?"

"Yes, although it was awkward when it happened. Which reminds me, I still owe you a ride around the ranch. Maybe while the boys are gone, we can schedule something. You can ride Daniel's horse."

"Isn't this your busy season? I don't want to interfere."

"Not too busy to keep my promises. I'll figure it out and let you know."

She began to collect the dirty dishes, to change the subject, he thought.

"You don't have to clean up. I'm good at doing dishes."

"You cooked..."

"I grilled. Guy stuff. Open flame. Red meat. That's not real cooking. I'll clean up." He took the dishes from her, and their hands brushed. Maybe it was the second beer he'd had. Maybe it was hearing the sympathy in her voice when they talked about his late wife. But the slight touch affected him more than a hug would have. He could feel emotions awaken that had been dormant for a long, long time, not to mention the usual reaction of a man when he's affected by a woman. Odd how discussing his late wife with her would elicit the response. Or maybe not so odd. Maybe thinking of the happy relationship he'd had with Paula for all those years made him realize what he was missing being alone.

He wondered if Quanna's stifled gasp meant she had felt it, too. Or maybe he'd merely startled her when he grabbed the plates.

"Actually, I should get home," she said. "I'm working the breakfast and lunch shift at the resort restaurant tomorrow and have to get there early."

"I thought you were taking a few days off."

"If I work extra shifts, I'll be able to take two classes this fall."

"All work and no play..."

"I'll take that chance."

He wanted to touch her again. Feel the jolt of electricity. But he didn't. All he did was dump the dirty dishes in the sink, walk her to her car, and tell her he'd see her on Tuesday.

After he loaded the dishwasher and cleaned up the kitchen, he went upstairs and did two things. First he went to his office, found the tax forms Quanna had filled out, and copied her address onto a Post-it note, which he tucked into his wallet. He wasn't sure what he intended to do with the information, but for some reason, he wanted to have it.

Next he went into his bedroom and picked up the photograph of his late wife that had been on his bureau for years. He brushed the back of his fingers over the image of her cheek, the way he used to touch her face. "Sam's right, Paula. You made me promise I wouldn't give up on life after you were gone. I guess it's time I live up to my promise. Wish me luck, darlin'. I'm out of practice at being romantic, something you always said I wasn't very good at anyway. I hope she's as patient with me as you were."

He took the photo out of the frame, went back to his office, and tucked it into a family album.

•••

All the way home, Quanna told herself the goose bumps Jack's touch had raised didn't mean anything. Except she knew they did, at least to her. She wasn't sure if the electricity she felt had registered with him. She couldn't expect he'd feel the same way about her. Although he had invited her to stay for dinner.

But that was probably so he'd have someone to eat with. After all, he was now alone in the house after two weeks of having four energetic boys around. Surely he just wanted a warm body and a little polite conversation. Although their conversation had become more intimate when they talked about Paula.

Intimate conversation. A warm body. His warm body was so very, very appealing. All she could think of while they were talking about his late wife was how much she wanted to comfort him. To hold him. Only hold him. Maybe kiss him. Not passionately. As a friend.

Liar. She didn't want to kiss him to comfort him. She wanted to find out what he tasted like. What it felt like to be in his arms. She was dangerously close to thinking it might be worth it to quit her job and find a way to connect more personally.

What stood in the way of throwing caution to the wind was simply that without full-time employment, she could never hope to finish her degree, which was tantalizingly close. And she couldn't contribute to the cost of the medical care her brother could only get in Portland. Not to mention the medications he needed for his heart problems.

Another obstacle was her relationship with Lucas and Daniel. How could she walk away from them? How could she be yet another mother figure who left?

Then there was the uneasy feeling that her Indian heritage might cause a few raised eyebrows in Jack's social circles. What would Doreen Campbell and her buddies think about Jack dating an Indian? Would Jack and the boys be the object of their scorn?

Besides, she wasn't exactly the most experienced seductress. Even if she decided to take a chance and try to get him to notice her, she wasn't sure she knew how to go about it. She'd had her share of dates but only one serious, adult relationship. Not exactly a record of triumphant conquests.

Caught up in the fantasy of being in Jack Richardson's arms and her quandary about whether to do something to make it happen, Quanna arrived at her building sooner than she expected, with little memory of the trip there. When she got into her apartment, she tried to read but that didn't work so well either. Neither did trying to get to sleep. Thoughts of Jack Richardson interfered with it all.

Monday morning, she arrived at the Wildhorse Resort on the reservation for her shift at 6:30 a.m. yawning. Thankfully, she was so busy she didn't have a chance to feel tired until she got to her car at three, after the lunch service was over. All she thought of on her way home was the long nap she had on her agenda as soon as she got in the door. A nap and forgetting about how attractive her boss was.

Chapter 8

There was no rational reason for Jack to head into Pendleton at seven o'clock on a Monday evening. He didn't need gas for the truck, supplies for his horses, or a part for the irrigation system. With the pantry and refrigerator stocked by Quanna, there was no reason to go to the grocery store. His usual day to see Aunt Joan was later in the week, and he didn't have a doctor or dentist appointment. Even so, he was on the road into town, his GPS set for an address on the Post-it note stuck to his dashboard.

How he was going to explain himself when he got to Quanna's apartment was also a mystery. What the hell was he going to say? There was no emergency. She hadn't left anything at the ranch that needed returning immediately. All he knew was that, somehow, after the conversation he'd had with his brother and the dinner he'd shared with her the night before, he wanted something from this woman. More than passing bits of conversation as he came and went, more than one dinner she'd made in his house like a lot of other evenings in the past few months. What that something was, he didn't quite know but he was on the road to see her and find out.

Fifteen miles into the drive from his ranch to town, the reasons not to do this hit him in rapid succession. Suppose she was offended by his chasing her to her home? What if she wasn't even home to be offended? He had no idea what her hours were at the casino restaurant. And even if she wasn't waitressing, she had a life outside working for him. She had a family she felt responsible for, among other demands, maybe classes to study for, if she was taking classes this summer. He didn't know if she was.

What if she was out? What if she was with a boyfriend? Did she have one? He didn't know that, either. He had never thought it was his place to ask. Lucas would probably know, but he hadn't thought to pump his son for information about his kid wrangler. How inappropriate would that be?

About as inappropriate as pursuing a woman over a decade younger than he was and who had become such an integral part of his kids' lives that he shouldn't even be thinking about what he was about to do. Yet here he was, potentially risking his boys' relationship with Quanna so he could see if she was interested in changing her relationship with him.

By the time he pulled into the parking lot of Quanna's apartment building, he'd tied himself in knots with "maybes," should Is," and "what ifs." When he saw her car parked close to the front door of the building, one knot loosened. It looked like she was home. He was relieved until it occurred to him she could have gone out in someone else's car. The knot returned.

Or, she could be home entertaining the boyfriend he didn't know she had. The knot tightened. It began to feel like a noose around his neck when he wondered, once again, if she'd be turned off by his being there.

He sat in his truck for several minutes trying to come up with some reason to see her. He wasn't sure he knew what he wanted other than to see her. He'd missed having her around the house all day, hearing her sing softly, talking to her when he had a chance even if the conversations were brief.

If he'd looked in the rearview mirror, he was sure he'd laugh at his furrowed brow and serious expression. How the hell had he gotten to this point? He was forty-four years old, had been running a million dollar wheat operation for decades, and he was sitting outside a rather shabby looking apartment building trying to decide if he should tuck his tail between his legs and go home or walk up to the building and talk to a woman.

Not being a coward—or being a fool, he wasn't sure which— he chose the latter.

The outer door wasn't locked. There was no buzzer to notify the residents someone had come into the building. Jack just walked up the internal steps. She was living someplace that wasn't very secure. Didn't that worry her?

He knocked on her door. From inside came the sound of Taylor Swift singing "Shake It Off," accompanied by Quanna. The song was Daniel and Lucas's favorite. And he didn't have to guess who had introduced them to it.

When his knock wasn't answered, he tried again, a bit louder. The music was apparently keeping her from hearing so he added "Quanna? It's Jack. Can you hear me?"

The music stopped, replaced shortly after by the sound of a chain lock being undone. Quanna opened the door with a worried expression on her face. "Jack? What're you doing here? Is something wrong?"

"This building isn't very safe," he said.

"So you're here to inspect the security arrangements where I live?"

He could feel the embarrassment begin to creep up his neck to his face. "No, sorry. That was rude."

She was smiling now. "Well, if it's not to evaluate my building, why are you here?"

"I just ... I don't know ... just wanted to..."

The door to the left of Quanna's opened with a bang, and an elderly man stepped out into the hall, interrupting Jack's fumbling explanation. The old man yelled, "I'm sick of listening to your noisy music and your loud friends, you cheap half-breed."

Jack immediately stood in front of Quanna, protecting her with his body, pushing her farther back into her apartment with one hand.

"Excuse me, what did you say?" Anger at the old man replaced his embarrassment.

"I said she's a half-breed tramp. Decent men don't have anything to do with her kind."

"I'll let what you said about me slide, but I suggest you apologize to Ms. Morales."

"Jack, please. Come in and forget it." Quanna pulled at his arm.

He hesitated, hearing the fear in her voice and not wanting to make it any worse. But when the old man sneered and said, "Got you whipped, does she? I hear they're pretty good in the sack," Jack moved.

In a few long strides he was at the man's front door, grabbing him by the shirtfront. "Old man, I was taught to respect my elders, but I'll make an exception in your case. Now, God damn it, apologize to Ms. Morales, or I'll show you what a whipping is."

"Think you're some sort of knight on a white horse, do you?"

Jack tightened his grip on the old man's shirt, which began to choke him. The man coughed, and Jack loosened his hold. "Apologize, damn it."

"Okay. Okay. If it means so much to you, I apologize."

"To her, not to me," Jack said.

"Sorry," the man said, looking at Quanna. Jack let go of him. The man stepped back into his apartment, slammed the door, and yelled, "Slut" at the top of his lungs.

Jack turned to see Quanna, ashen-faced and shaking. She motioned him in from the hall, gulping back tears.

He didn't fight his instinct to comfort her. As soon as he was in the apartment, he had his arms around her, murmuring, "It's okay. I won't let him hurt you."

"It's not me I'm worried about. He could have hurt *you*," she said as she slumped against him.

"I'm bigger and in better shape. He couldn't do anything to me."

"He has a gun, Jack. I didn't know if he had it on him."

For several minutes, they stood in an embrace, he soothing her with soft sounds and gentle touches, she stifling her tears with deep breathing. On one last shuddery sigh, she pulled away from him. "Thanks. I'm okay now. Embarrassed but okay."

"Your neighbor's the one who should be embarrassed, not you." As he closed and locked the front door, he was already missing the warmth of her against his chest. "Has he done shit like this before?" he asked. When she nodded, he said, "You shouldn't have to put up with it. Have you complained to the building manager?"

Waving off his suggestion with a vague gesture, she replied, "I ignore him when he rants."

"If you thought he might hurt me, how do you know he won't try to hurt you?"

"I don't grab him by the shirt and threaten to beat him up. He's a crabby old man who hates Indians. That's all."

Jack raked his fingers through his hair, furious and frustrated he couldn't figure out how to make it better. "Surely there must be something..."

"Can we forget him for now? I'd rather get back to the conversation we were having when he interrupted." Quanna had gone to the opposite side of the room, as if to put space between them. She was quiet and still, her brown eyes huge. "You never answered the question about why you're here." She sounded apprehensive.

"Okay, but we're not finished talking about him." He looked around, hoping there was something to help him explain the inexplicable. "Nothing's wrong. At least, nothing you've done. It's me." He saw fear cross her face again. "No, no, I didn't mean it that way. There's nothing wrong with me either. I don't know how to explain it. I'm not sure I should be here. I'm too old for this sort of thing. Or you're too young. Whichever. You should be out with people your own age, some young guy who can ... I don't know ... do the things you like to do. Not some old fart like me with a couple of kids and a lot of baggage."

"I'm not clear what 'this sort of thing' is." The fear in her eyes had begun to disappear. She seemed more curious now, maybe even amused. She began to move closer to him.

"And then there's the whole awkwardness about you working for me. I don't want you to feel obligated or anything. Don't want things to be uncomfortable for you. God knows, the kids would kill me if something I did messed up the arrangement with you."

"I agree. We don't want to make things awkward." She took another step toward him. "But what is it you think might do that?" She looked like she was fighting a smile as she prodded him to talk.

"I don't know why this is so hard. Well, that's not true. I do know. I'm not sure it's the right thing to do. And I'm not good at it. Never have been. All I know is, it's what I want to do."

Now she was standing directly in front of him. She put her hand on his arm. "So, what is it you want to do, Jack?"

"Dinner. I thought maybe we could have dinner again. I enjoyed last night. I like talking with you. Could we, would you be interested in doing the same thing again? Only this time, maybe go someplace where neither one of us has to cook."

She was beaming now, her whole face lit up with pleasure. "I'd love to have dinner with you. But let me cook. Maybe at the ranch so we don't run into my awful neighbor again."

"I want this to be different from what you do every day at the house. I want to take you out. I know some good places in town where I think you might..."

"You don't know what you're letting yourself in for. My neighbor's not alone in his opinions. Remember those two jerks in the bar?" The fear was beginning to creep back into her eyes, and her smile had dimmed.

"That was unusual. You won't hear that anyplace I'd take you."

"Unfortunately, that's not true. I don't want you to have people looking at you the way he did because you're with me. I'll cook."

He knew she could be stubborn. He'd seen her with the boys when she was trying to get them to do something they didn't want to do. Apparently, however, she didn't realize how stubborn he could be. He took her hand in both of his. "If you don't want to go to a restaurant in Pendleton, how about the one where you work? I want to take you out to dinner, and I'm not going to let some old bigot change my plans."

"I would have said the same thing even if he hadn't come out of his lair. There are people like him all over the place."

"I hate to think anyone would say ugly things to you. To anyone, but especially to you." He put his arm around her shoulders and pulled her to his side. Bad move on his part. Now that he had her close to him again, he wanted to draw her even nearer and finally see what she tasted like. *Get on with the conversation, Richardson, before you do something stupid. Like kiss her.* "You didn't answer about going to the restaurant at the casino."

He felt her sigh.

"I guess it would work. If you're sure you want to do this."

"I'm positive." He released her. "So it's settled. Dinner at the casino restaurant." She nodded. For the first time, he noticed the circles under her eyes. "You look tired. You've had a long day. I'm sorry I barged in. I thought it would be better to do this outside your work hours and in person. But now I'll get out of your way."

"You're not in my way. I was reading for a class I hope to take this fall."

"You and Taylor Swift?" It was his turn to smile knowingly.

"Oh, right. You heard. Well, taking a break from reading actually."

"I'll let you get back to it." He opened the front door. "I apologize for the scene in the hall. You should report your neighbor, you know."

"I'm not going to make waves. I have to live here."

"Your call. But promise me, if he gets bad again, you'll do something about it."

He waited for her to nod, which she did, barely.

"Okay, then I'll see you tomorrow at the house." He started to leave, but she touched his arm.

"Wait. We agreed on dinner but not when."

He shook his head and smiled. "Shows you how out of practice I am. How about Wednesday night? That work for you?"

"Perfect. And, yes, I'll see you tomorrow at the ranch."

• • •

Of course she couldn't get to sleep after he left. He had defended her, comforted her, asked her out. The pleasure of being in his arms as he held her had been better than any of her fantasies. It made her want more. Now that she knew what it was like to be held by him, she wanted to know what it would be like to kiss him. God only knows what she'd want after that.

Eventually her weariness from the previous night's insomnia, a long, full day at the restaurant, and the emotional confrontation with her neighbor won out, and she fell into a deep sleep. Once there, the dreams she had prominently featured a sexy cowboy wearing a white hat like some old black and white movie. He rode to her rescue on an Appaloosa, scooping her up from the midst of a crowd carrying torches and nooses, then riding off with her. She woke up smiling at some point, only to go back to sleep and continue the adventure.

The next morning, instead of throwing on the first pair of jeans she could find and the cleanest T-shirt in her drawer, she dressed more carefully, making sure the jeans she selected fit her well and hunting down the coral color knit top she knew was flattering to her coloring. Before she left for the ranch, she put her freshly washed hair in a perfect braid and even slapped on a bit of lipstick to match her shirt.

But as she drove down the road to the house, she could see Jack's truck was missing. He was out someplace. Her careful preparations had been in vain.

The lipstick had been chewed off, and the knit shirt had collected a few spots by the end of the day, which was when Jack arrived back at the house. He offered her a glass of wine, which she turned down, peeked into the oven to see what she'd left him for dinner, and asked if six was a good time to pick her up the following night. He was warm and friendly, as he usually was, and there was no mention of the incident of the day before.

She wasn't sure if she was relieved or disappointed.

Chapter 9

Quanna's shift at the restaurant on Wednesday dragged so badly she swore she'd worked eighteen hours instead of eight. Feeling like a school kid released for summer vacation when she was finally finished, she raced home to shower and change. When she looked through her closet for something to wear, once again, she regretted not having enough money to buy a nicer wardrobe. There was no floaty, girly skirt or silky top, no sundress with a halter neckline, no sandals with a web of straps to hold them on her feet.

Instead, she was stuck with the same old clothes: regular jeans or ripped jeans, a couple pairs of knit pants, her scrubs from her job at Golden Years, her restaurant uniform, athletic shoes, boots, and ballet flats.

Finally she decided on a pair of new, never-worn jeans paired with a little top she'd forgotten she owned until she found it in the back of her closet. It was a totally impractical thing she'd bought in Portland for a date with the guy she'd been seeing. A warm beige color that looked good with her skin, the top consisted of four layers of fluttery gauze. Hanging from two thin spaghetti straps, it barely reached her waist. Not the floaty skirt she wanted, but the way the gauze layers moved around her torso was almost as good.

A wide belt and her dressier boots accessorized her choices. She added the little bit of makeup she wore—her coral lipstick—and she was ready to go. At five-thirty.

If she thought her work shift had crept by slowly, the half hour until Jack was due moved with a speed that made a glacier look like Road Runner.

Finally, at five of six, there was a knock at the door. When she opened it, Jack was shifting his weight back and forth from one boot-shod foot to the other, as if he were nervous. Thinking maybe he was a little anxious about this, too, settled her down somewhat. The deep breath she took to calm herself gave her a whiff of the familiar smell of his sage-y soap, which also helped. He, too, was in jeans as crisp and new looking as hers were. His white shirt set off his tan face handsomely. She was pretty sure he was freshly shaved.

Clearing his throat, he handed her a bouquet of wildflowers wrapped in brown paper and said, "Hi," his voice a bit higher than usual. He coughed again before continuing in a more normal tone. "I brought these for you. You've said you like the plains so I figured you'd like wildflowers. Thought maybe you'd like to have them in your apartment to remind you of what's outside the city."

She took the bouquet and touched the coneflowers and lupine before smiling and saying, "I do love them. Thank you." She gestured for him to sit down. "Let me get them in water before we go."

• • •

Jack couldn't remember when he'd felt less sure of himself. It was worse than when he was in high school. Of course, then he'd had a steady girlfriend and only had to worry about grades and getting into college. He didn't have to be anxious about how an evening out would go. Like he was tonight.

He watched Quanna rummage through a kitchen cabinet until she found a clear glass vase, the kind a million florists use. Someone had sent her flowers at one time or another, he'd bet. He wondered if she'd smiled at the guy's flowers the way she'd smiled at the ones he brought her. That other guy couldn't have known to give her wildflowers if he sent her something from a florist. He congratulated himself on being smarter than the other guy.

What the hell was he thinking? He was stupidly jealous of some nameless, faceless guy who wasn't around anymore. But would anyone blame him? She looked beautiful. She was wearing some little bit of a top that made it obvious, without looking trashy, there wasn't a bra underneath. The fabric of the shirt-top-whatever-it-was moved gently around her as she trimmed the stems of the flowers, stripped off some of the leaves, and arranged them in the vase.

And then there was the view he was getting of her rear end in those jeans that fit like a glove.

Stop. He had to stop thinking of how good her body looked. If he didn't, he'd be drooling like some old guy looking at the swimsuit edition of *Sports Illustrated* before they got out of the place. He had to find something else to look at, to talk about. Something. Anything.

At first glance, there wasn't much to distract him. Her apartment was a small studio with only the bare essentials. He was sitting on a futon he was sure doubled as her bed, which was another direction he had to steer his thoughts clear of. The only other furniture was a wooden rocking chair and a small bistro-style wrought iron table with two chairs. The kitchen was across the room from where he was sitting, and a door next to it led, he assumed, to the bathroom.

In spite of the tiny space, however, it was not boring once he began to look more closely. Quanna had surrounded herself with color—pillows and a throw on the futon, a rug under the small table, and a curtain swagged over the window, all in shades of brown and sage green, soft orange and gold. Displayed on a small bookcase along with what looked like textbooks were two baskets and a piece of beadwork. Probably created by modern Umatilla artisans. On the wall were photos of Eastern Oregon landscapes, like some of the work in his house.

"I didn't notice much about your apartment when I was here on Monday," he said. "It looks nice. I like it."

She smiled. "Thanks. Most of it is from the room I had in Portland. I missed the colors of home and decorated it to remind me." She pointed to the photos. "My brother Frank took those pictures and had them blown up for me as a present when I said I was homesick for the plains."

"He's a good photographer."

"He'd like to sell more of his work, but he's got kids to raise. So he works for the tribe, running the campgrounds near the resort, while he does his photography on the side."

"He should keep at it. He's got a good eye."

"I'll tell him you said so." She put the vase on the small bistro table. "Thank you again for these. I love wildflowers. Better than cultivated flowers, actually." She dried her hands on a cloth towel and looked around as if trying to see what else needed to be done. "I guess that's it. I'm ready to go if you are."

• • •

She had warned her coworkers she'd be back with a date, but when they got to the resort, Jack didn't head for the Traditions buffet where she worked. Instead, he guided her to Plateau, the fine dining restaurant where she'd never eaten. She wasn't sure if she should suggest they go to the other restaurant or keep her mouth shut and enjoy the luxury of the place she'd heard such good things about from her coworkers.

As if he were reading her mind, Jack said, "I never asked which restaurant you worked in but decided I'd make a reservation at the one I've never been in. I've eaten at Traditions but not here." He pulled out the chair for her to be seated.

"I've never eaten here either. Traditions is where I work."

After a few minutes of perusing the menu, he asked, "Have you heard what's good?"

"The salmon is good in both restaurants. I hear the whiskey steak is delicious."

"I usually prefer my own steak, but the buffalo Bolognese looks interesting."

"Which no Italian would claim, I'm sure," she said, laughing.

Their server interrupted and asked if they'd like to order drinks. When she turned to take Quanna's order, her eyes widened. "Quanna! I didn't recognize you at first."

"Hi, Kimi."

Kimi looked back and forth between Quanna and Jack. Finally Quanna said, "This is Jack Richardson. Jack, this is Kimi Miller. We worked together at Traditions until she got the job here."

Glasses of wine were ordered and the specials recited. A somewhat awkward silence fell when Kimi left.

"Are you uncomfortable being seen with me?" Jack asked.

"Uncomfortable? No. I can't imagine why you'd think I am."

"You're quieter than usual. I thought maybe you were uneasy being out with someone so much older than you are."

"I don't know how old you are, so I couldn't be uneasy about your age."

"I'm sixteen years older than you are. That's quite a span."

"So it makes you uncomfortable." She waved off the objection she was sure was coming. "I'm a lot older than my chronologic years, Jack. Your age isn't an issue."

Their wine arrived, and he tilted his glass toward hers so they could touch the rims together and toast. "Cheers. Thank you for agreeing to this," he said.

"I should be thanking you." She took a sip of her wine. "Even the wine tastes better here."

He laughed. "Probably because it's a higher quality than the kind I gave you the other night."

They ordered salmon for her and buffalo Bolognese for him. Both, it turned out, delicious. The conversation over their entrees was mostly about what the boys were doing in Portland and how the wheat crop looked for the season. But when their dinner plates were cleared and they waited for their desserts, Jack returned to the conversation they'd started before dinner.

"I'm curious about what you said—about being older than your years. I realize I don't know a whole lot about you other than the glowing references I got from everyone who ever employed you. And the clean criminal background check I got."

"You did a criminal background check on me?" She wasn't sure if she should be angry or surprised.

"I would have done it for anyone I was leaving in charge of my kids. Didn't you have to have one at Golden Years?"

"Yes, but I never thought I'd have to have one to work in someone's home."

"It was important to know my kids were safe."

"I understand. I shouldn't have sounded so surprised."

"Or angry."

"Yeah, a little bit." She picked up a spoon and stared intently at it, twisting it in her fingers. "I've heard too many times how Indians can't be trusted. I'd like people to trust me."

"And I do. With what I value most—my two boys." He reached across the table and took the spoon from her hand. "Are you avoiding talking about your personal life? If you are, that's okay. It's not any of my business."

"Of course it's your business. I practically live in your house. It's just that my family's not particularly interesting."

"Why would you say that? Your mom's Umatilla. You told the boys the first time you met them your dad was from Central America. There must be an interesting story about how they met."

"He came through here as migrant labor and stayed when they fell in love. They got married and proceeded to have a bunch of kids. He had very little education so work was hard to find. We never had much money. I don't think he ever considered himself a success at much of anything. Not like you and your family." She was trying hard not to sound defensive about her family, but it wasn't easy. Compared to Jack and his siblings and their family ranch, her family wasn't very successful.

"Do you speak both your parents' languages?"

"Not as well as either my mother or father would have liked, but I can get along in Umatilla and I'm pretty good with Spanish."

"Did—does—your mom work outside the house?"

"She doesn't. Miguel, the youngest of my siblings, was born with Down syndrome and a congenital heart problem. He needs full-time care."

"So, two brothers ..."

"And a sister, Aiyana. She's the oldest. Then Frank, me, and Miguel."

"How come Frank doesn't have an interesting name like the rest of you?"

She laughed. "He's actually Franco. The boys got Hispanic names like our dad. The two girls got Indian names like our mom."

"As long as I'm prying into your life, mind if I ask something else?"

"Of course not."

"What made you move to Portland? You lived there for quite a while even though you said you love the plains."

"My mom wanted both her daughters away from here so we wouldn't end up like her, no education, early marriage, bunch of kids. Aiyana went to Bellingham to live with a cousin while she went to school to be a nurse. I thought Portland was a better choice for me to get my degree so I could teach."

"You moved back before you finished. How come?"

"It was hard to make enough money to live in Portland and go to school while I was working full-time shift work. And the boyfriend who I thought might be serious someday broke up with me about the same time my dad died. It seemed a good time to move back and help my mom."

"I can only take so much of the city. I admire you for sticking it out for all those years. I can't make it through much more than a weekend." He sat back in his chair and began to play with the spoon he'd taken away from her. "Can you get the degree you want from Blue Mountain?"

"Maybe. I'm working with them to see what we can do with the credits I have, the classes they teach, and their transfer program. We'll see."

"Anything I can do to help?"

"You already have. You gave me a full-time job. It's not only the best job I've ever had, but because of you, I didn't have to give up my apartment and move back into my mother's home."

"Sounds like you do more for your family than you do for yourself."

"I wouldn't say that. I have friends. I go to school. All I ever wanted to do was teach, and I'm getting there. Slowly, more slowly than anyone on record, I imagine, but I'm getting there."

"What'll you do when you get your teaching certificate?"

"Teach on the rez. American Indians have the lowest high school graduation rates of any group in the country. I want to work to change that."

"If you need more time off for classes so you can get there faster, we can work out a better schedule."

"That's generous of you, but you already do more than I could hope for."

Finally, dessert arrived and she could concentrate on eating chocolate and not on the concern she saw in his eyes as she talked about her family. She didn't need to feel any closer to or warmer about the man sitting across from her, the man who was growing more attractive by the minute and not because she'd had a glass of wine.

• • •

Jack couldn't remember the last time he'd enjoyed a meal as much as he was enjoying this one. Hell, he couldn't remember the last time he'd done something social with anyone other than his kids or his siblings. Somehow this evening, it didn't seem to matter that he was older than she was, that he was her employer. She was a beautiful woman and he was a man, and they were enjoying each other's company and a good dinner. He wanted it to go on forever. Although he thought it might be a good idea if he let her lead the conversation for a while instead of quizzing her like he'd been doing.

He couldn't get his wish that the evening not end. Eventually, the check arrived, and they had to leave. They both worked the next day. But he was determined to make sure they didn't part without making plans for seeing each other again outside her job. He decided to ask her when they said good night.

It didn't quite work out the way he'd planned.

When they got to her apartment building, she unhooked her seatbelt and started to open the door. "Thank you so much for a lovely dinner."

"I should be thanking you. If you hadn't agreed to dinner with me, I would have been all alone, missing my boys."

"It does seem weird in the house without them, doesn't it?"

"You miss them, too?"

"Of course I do. They're amazing kids. You've done a great job raising them."

"And you're doing a great job with them."

"On that note of mutual admiration, I better go upstairs." She got the car door opened before he could stop her.

"Wait. Let me walk you upstairs."

"I'm fine, Jack. I do this every day."

"Maybe you do. But I'm still walking you to the door. Between your asshole neighbor and no security on the front door, I'm not leaving you until I know you're safe."

She rolled her eyes. "Okay, I give up. You can walk up the steps with me."

When they got to her front door, she unlocked it and put out her hand to him, making it clear she had a handshake in mind and started, he assumed, to say good night again. He had other ideas. Taking her proffered hand, he clasped it to his chest. With the backs of the curled fingers of his free hand he touched her cheek. "I don't think I've ever met anyone who is as strong and levelheaded as you are. I admire you for your persistence in going to school and what you're doing for your family."

"I'm flattered by your compliment, especially since it comes from the man rumor says is the most responsible person for three counties." He was sure she was trying to lighten what had become an atmosphere heavy with the chemistry between the two of them.

"The rumor came from ...?"

"Your aunt, of course."

"Ah, I should have guessed." He ran his thumb over her lower lip and took a step closer to her, still holding her hand.

• • •

He was going to kiss her. She was absolutely sure he was going to kiss her. She'd spent the whole ride home from the restaurant wondering if he would try. And how she would react. Now she knew. He was going to try, and she was going to let him.

With one hand, she could feel his heartbeat, how it had kicked up a notch when he touched her face, pounded even harder when he rubbed her mouth. Her heartbeat wasn't far behind.

When he moved closer to her, she swore she could feel waves of heat shimmering between them, warming her body, melting her insides. It didn't matter anymore whether this was a good idea or not. It was going to happen. She wanted it to happen.

He released her hand and took her face in both of his hands. His dark brown eyes were pools of desire, drawing her in. Without thinking, she moved closer to him, so their bodies were only inches apart.

"Jack ..." she began, sure she moaned his name rather than spoke it.

However it came out, it seemed to break the spell between them. He dropped his hands and took a step back. "I ... I guess I better go. We both have to work in the morning."

"Right. Work." She took a breath to settle her nerves. "Thanks again. It was lovely."

He smiled, that huge grin she loved, and was gone.

She closed the door and stood motionless for a few seconds. What had happened? He'd been about to kiss her; she was sure. But he didn't. Why? Was it the whole employer/employee thing? Was he still worried about her age? Had she had too much garlic with her dinner?

She'd probably never know.

Chapter 10

After his hasty exit from the kiss at her front door, Jack sat in his truck wanting to pound his head on the steering wheel for being so lame. When the impulse passed, he started the engine but couldn't make himself drive off. He didn't want to go home. Not yet. Why had he screwed up his attempt to kiss her good night when it was obvious she was willing? What was he afraid of?

He turned the engine off, jumped out of his truck, and headed for the building. As he took the steps two at a time, he realized that if he were smart, he should probably haul ass back to his truck. But there was little evidence that anything related to what he was doing with this woman showed how smart he was.

After he knocked, the door opened wide enough for him to see she was surprised. "Jack? Did you forget something?" She looked back over her shoulder as if to see what he'd left behind.

"Yeah, I guess you can say I forgot something." He raked his fingers through his hair. "Can I come in?"

"Oh. Right. Sure." She opened the door all the way to let him in.

"I didn't leave anything. That's not why I came back." He took two steps toward her, got close enough to smell her spicy, vanilla scent, see her brown eyes widen, and hear the sharp intake of breath as she registered how near he'd come to her. "I'm here because there're a couple things I meant to do before I left."

Before she could ask any more questions, he put his hands on her shoulders and drew her to him. "The first thing I meant to do was this." He lowered his head and touched his mouth to hers. It took all the discipline he could muster to keep from crushing her against him and kissing her with everything he'd been trying to hide, to control, for the past months. He was sure his hands were shaking with the effort.

But he needed her to want the kiss as much as he did. He wanted to persuade her, not pounce on her. When she relaxed against him, he knew he'd done the right thing.

The soft, almost weightless kisses he trailed from her mouth to her jaw and down to the pulse in her throat, elicited a soft moan from her, and her arms went around his neck. Taking it as a sign she wanted the kiss, too, he returned to her mouth, nipped at her bottom lip, then, with the tip of his tongue, explored the seam of her lips.

She responded by opening to him, letting him deepen the kiss. His tongue explored her mouth, joined with her tongue in a slick, sliding, sensuous dance. She pressed herself against him; he couldn't hide the evidence of his arousal. Didn't want to hide it any longer. He wanted her to know exactly what she did to him.

For what seemed to be long minutes, they stood locked in an embrace while they learned the taste and texture of each other's mouth and while their bodies began to find the ways they fit together.

She broke from the kiss first. Although she kept her arms around his neck and her body pressed against his, she drew back far enough to take a deep breath.

He needed to have more contact with her so he touched his forehead to hers. "Should I apologize for that?"

She smiled. "Not unless you think you didn't do it right."

"I'll let you decide if I did or didn't." He kissed the tip of her nose. "But keep in mind, I've been out of practice for a while. Although from the way it took me two tries to actually kiss you, you probably figured that out."

"I find it hard to believe you're out of practice when you're so good at it."

"I've wanted to kiss you for weeks. But I wasn't sure if I should. I mean, I don't want you to feel awkward about it."

"Awkward isn't the word I'd use to describe how I feel right now."

Since he could feel the hard tips of her breasts against his chest and the rest of her body continued to be pressed against his, he thought he might know how she felt. Still, he wanted to hear her say the words to let him know she liked it. "How do you feel?" he asked.

"Happy. I've wanted this for weeks, too."

With every word she spoke, his anxiety faded even more.

"You said there were two things you forgot," she continued. "After the first one, I'm curious about the second."

"Right. The other thing. I was wondering if you're working Friday."

"Oh. You want to know my work schedule." She dropped her gaze to focus on his shirt buttons. A slight crease appeared between her eyebrows.

She was disappointed at what he'd said. Which made him unaccountably glad.

"Did you expect something else?"

"I wondered ... I thought ... never mind. It's not important." She looked up and shrugged one shoulder, as if to be nonchalant. Her expression, which looked disappointed, belied the gesture.

He was tempted to keep her in suspense, rather enjoying having her off balance instead of feeling off balance himself. But it would be too cruel. "I thought, if you weren't busy, I could give you the tour of the ranch you got cheated out of when Daniel threw his hissy fit. Then maybe we could, I don't know, grab a bite to eat?"

Her smile returned like the sun after a summer thundershower. "Are you trying to fatten me up for some reason? All you seem to want to do is feed me."

"That's not it. I don't know what you like to do, and since we both have to eat ..."

"You know I'm teasing you, don't you? And to answer your question, I'm working the breakfast and lunch shifts on Friday. I'm finished about three."

"Why don't you come out to the ranch about five, then? We can ride for a couple hours and figure out dinner."

"Don't you have to help harvest somewhere?"

"I should be finished by four, four-thirty. Then I'm free." He ducked his head and lightly kissed her mouth. "So I'll see you at five on Friday."

Before he could get to the door, she said, "You mean you'll see me tomorrow, don't you?"

"Tomorrow? Oh, right. Of course. I'll see you tomorrow." He closed the door before she could react so he didn't have to see if she was laughing at him for not remembering she was working at the ranch the next day. Because he knew as well as she did, what had made him forgetful was their kiss.

He jumped into the cab of his truck but didn't start the engine right away. He hadn't been adept at asking Quanna out, but what did you expect from a man who had only asked one woman for a date since middle school? In the end, he had not only asked her out twice but he had even managed to kiss her. That, at least, he was confident he'd done right, assuming he was judging her reaction correctly.

He turned the key in the ignition, put the truck into gear, and headed for the road home. Both he and his truck were on a roll.

• • •

Not for the first time, Quanna was nervous driving to the Richardson Ranch. Before it had been about the impression she would make on a potential employer. Now it was about how it would go with Jack after the night before. It was obvious things had changed between them. The dinner date alone and how cute he'd been when he asked her out would have made that evident. But adding the kiss? Big-time change. The kiss was ... well, it was "too" everything. Too amazing. Too serious. Too much what she wanted. Too likely to make it difficult to be around him without wanting a repeat.

The question wasn't whether things had changed. It was how much they had changed and, more importantly, for how long and with what consequences. She had fought the attraction for weeks, sure she'd endanger the job that meant so much to her security if she acted. But when he'd kissed her, all thoughts of the job disappeared. She wanted this man in a way she'd never wanted any man before. And if his kiss and his reaction to her were any indication, he wanted her the same way.

He was an honorable man, an honest man, who had been as worried about what it could mean as she was. He'd never do anything to make her feel insecure. The fact he had been so open about what it might mean said volumes about who he was. She trusted him.

Still. After the night before, how would they react to each other when they were back in the boss/employee mode?

She was about to find out.

Except she didn't, at least not at first. Once again, Jack was gone when she got to the house. She accomplished the few things she had to do, roasted a chicken and made a pasta salad for dinner for him, and was about to gather up the things she'd left by the front door and leave when she heard the distinctive sound of his truck tires crunching on the gravel drive. In spite of her resolve not to let him affect her, her heartbeat kicked up a notch or two as she watched from the kitchen window while he hopped down from the cab of the truck and sauntered toward the back door. When he knocked on the hood of her car and flashed a huge grin she realized he knew she was watching.

"I was afraid you'd be gone by the time I got back from my sister's place," he said as he toed off his boots in the mudroom. "I'm glad I didn't miss you. I wanted to ask you to stay and have dinner with me. Assuming you don't have class or anything planned for tonight, I mean."

She'd never realized how sexy sock feet and worn jeans could be on a man. But then, she imagined he'd look sexy to her in sweatpants and flip-flops, basketball shorts and sneakers, or a trash bag and hiking boots. "Feeding me again?" she teased.

"Eat. Don't eat. Doesn't matter. As long as you keep me company while I eat. I've been thinking about dinner and you all day, although not in that order most of the time."

She couldn't help it. His words warmed her to her core. "I'd love to stay. Let me know when you want to eat, and I'll finish getting things ready."

"Now works for me. I'm starving. We ate lunch on the run so we could get everything done today. And although I love my sister, her healthy sandwiches leave a lot to be desired."

Quanna pulled out the bowl of pasta salad, the makings of a green salad, and the chicken she'd finished up earlier in the day. While she plated their dinners, Jack washed up and put on his Nikes, hiding his sexy sock feet. Just as well. The rest of his sexiness was still quite visible and unnerving.

"So, did you get everything finished at your sister's place?" she asked after they were settled at the table.

"Yup. Her wheat is in. Then the Wilsons, the Salazars, and Doreen Campbell. I'm at the end of the line."

"Good crop this year?"

"Not bad. Price isn't what we hoped for, but then, it never is." He had cleared the food from his plate so fast Quanna had no doubts about how hungry he had been.

She reached for his plate. "Let me get you seconds."

"I can do it." He started to brush her hand off his plate, but when their fingers connected, the jolt she felt was considerable. He must have felt it, too, because he looked up, his eyes all pupil. But he didn't pull his hand away. "I should know better, shouldn't I? Touching you does the damnedest things to me." He squeezed her hand before picking up his plate and heading for the kitchen.

She was left speechless, completely uninterested in food, and feeling almost as high as if she had been drinking wine.

• • •

It wasn't until he saw the pile of pasta salad he'd mindlessly heaped on his plate that Jack realized he wasn't paying attention to what he was doing. In fact, he was thinking, again, as he had been all day, about the kiss from the night before. The zing of electricity that had hit him when their hands had touched just now reminded him of how powerful it had been.

He returned half the salad to the serving bowl, added a couple slices of chicken to his plate, and took a few moments to compose himself. Then he returned to the dining room. Quanna was picking at her food.

"Did I insist on eating too early?"

"No, the time's fine. I guess I tasted too much while I was cooking. I'm not very hungry."

She wasn't looking directly at him, which was unusual for her. And he was pretty sure she'd tucked into the food with enthusiasm when they'd first sat down at the table.

She was reacting to the connection they'd just felt, and he was glad.

Later, he couldn't remember what they talked about for the rest of the meal. All he knew was he ate his second plateful of food and Quanna eventually ate most of what she'd dished up for herself. They cleared away the dishes when they were finished, and he loaded the dishwasher while she made a pot of coffee.

She was fussing with mugs and the sugar bowl when she said, "Do you mind if I ask you a personal question?"

"Fire away." He couldn't think of anything she could ask that would be too intrusive to answer.

"When I was putting clean towels in the bathroom upstairs, I noticed the picture on your bureau is gone. Why did you move it?" She turned around to look at him while he answered.

The question was surprising, although it shouldn't have been. He was sure she knew exactly where everything in the house was. "I put it away when I got back from Portland." He shrugged. "My brother said something to me when I was there about knowing when it was time to move on. I've been at that point for a while now, but I hadn't done anything about it. Didn't have a reason to, I guess." He stopped before he could talk himself into a corner he wasn't sure he was ready to be in yet.

"But the boys ..."

"The photos of Paula with the kids are still around and will be. But that one, well, I needed to let it go."

"Even though it's still her room, too?"

"The one thing I did after she died was to completely redo the bedroom. I couldn't face sleeping in what had been a sickroom and a deathbed, but I didn't want to change rooms. I moved out all the furniture, repainted, bought a new bed and linens. Made it only and completely mine." He tried to control the grin that was threatening to break out at the thought that she cared about this particular subject. "That answer your question?"

"Yes. Thank you. I apologize for being curious."

"You shouldn't. If anyone has a right to know, you do."

He expected her to ask why he thought she had the right, but she didn't. Instead, she poured coffee. Without asking, she added the two sugars he took in his before handing him the mug.

"About tomorrow ..." she began.

"I thought we'd ride around the ranch for a couple hours then have a picnic dinner out by the pond." He motioned to her to follow him into the living room where they settled onto the couch.

"What can I contribute to dinner?" she asked.

He laughed. "I think you've got it covered already. I was planning on bringing whatever you've left in the refrigerator for me."

"I could bake brownies. Or chocolate chip cookies, if you'd like."

"Now who's trying to fatten up whom? Thanks, but the fruit in the kitchen will be fine. Save the brownies and cookies to bribe the boys when they come home."

"Did you hear from them today? What are they up to?" she asked.

While they finished their coffee, he gave her a report on his sons' latest activities. She seemed relieved at the less emotional topic of conversation. When the report was over and the coffee cups were empty, she started to gather them up, saying, "I better get home. My day starts early tomorrow."

"Don't worry about the dishes. I'll take care of them." He extended his hand to her. "Let me walk you out."

She took his hand, and once again, he felt the tingle of contact with her. He reluctantly let go of her so she could collect her purse and a light jacket she'd left on the bench in the entry. As soon as she was ready to leave, he took her hand again, gently rubbing his thumb over hers as they walked to her car.

"See you tomorrow after your shift," he said.

"Yes. And thanks for dinner."

"Which you prepared," he reminded her.

"With your food. In your kitchen."

"Is this a competition?" he asked, amused at her insistence about the meal.

"No. It's a reality check about who's responsible for what around here."

He ducked his head and kissed her, drawing her against him where he knew she would feel his beginning arousal. "No, *that's* a reality check. About who does what to whom." Raising their still entwined hands, he kissed the tips of her fingers.

Her face was soft with emotion. Her eyes were huge, dark pools that tempted him to dive in. She swallowed hard and slipped her hand from his. "I better go."

He nodded. "Yes. You better. See you tomorrow."

He watched until her car was out of sight then returned to the house, which was once again empty. Of life and warmth and music. Of his boys.

Empty of Quanna, which he was beginning to think was the biggest void of them all.

Chapter 11

Jack was unloading bales of hay from the bed of his pickup when Quanna arrived on Friday. He leaned against the side of the truck and watched her walk toward him, enjoying the sway of her hips and the swing of her braid. She was in jeans, as usual, but today, instead of a T-shirt, she wore a long-sleeved shirt, the shirttails tied around her slender waist. She looked beautiful. But then, no matter what she wore, she was without doubt the most beautiful woman he'd had the pleasure of watching in a long, long time.

"Hi, there." She nodded toward the bales of hay. "Want some help?"

"Hi, back. Thanks for the offer, but they're pretty heavy. I don't want you to hurt yourself."

She vaulted into the bed of the truck and went to the nearest bale. "Don't let my size fool you. I'm a lot stronger than I look." With an efficient movement, she hoisted the hay and dropped it into Jack's arms. He grunted at the impact. She grinned.

With two of them working, it didn't take long to unload the truck and move the bales into the barn where the five Appaloosas were stabled.

They saddled two of the horses. Quanna was to ride Daniel's horse, Paint, which Jack assured her had been cleared with his son.

When the horses were ready, Jack pulled his Stetson off a peg and drew it down onto his forehead. "Don't you have something for your head? The sun's pretty brutal today."

"I meant to bring a hat but forgot."

He grabbed a baseball cap from another peg. "I'll loan you one." He reached around her and pulled her braid through the hole in the back of the cap before settling it on her head. She drew a shaky breath as he patted the cap into place. His breath wasn't exactly steady. If he didn't take a step back, there wouldn't be a ride. There would be a roll in the hay they'd just brought in.

He looked around, trying to find something to take his mind off the hay and the woman in front of him. Gloves. He'd get her some gloves. He nabbed a pair, dropped one, picked it up, and offered them to her. "Want these? They're an extra pair of mine so they'll be a bit big. But the kids' would be too small. Afraid we don't have any that're just right, Goldilocks."

"These'll do, Papa Bear. Anything else I need?"

He picked up two sets of saddlebags and handed one to her. "For our dinner," he said.

"A lot of food for two people, isn't it?" She seemed to realize as she put the saddlebags on the horse, hers weren't heavy. "Or maybe not."

"You're carrying the blanket and pillows. In case one of us needs a nap. Or something," he said as he mounted Hero. He waited for her to mount Paint then tugged on the reins to direct his horse to the road up from the ranch. Quanna followed.

Soon they were riding between fields of ripe wheat and ripening alfalfa, spotting the occasional sage grouse trying to hide from the hawks hunting them. The only sounds were of the birds and the muted thump of distant wind turbines. They said little, merely rode and enjoyed the experience.

At the bottom of a small hill, Jack halted his horse in the shade of a cottonwood tree. "I need a slug of water. How about you?" he asked, grabbing the metal canteen hooked around his saddle horn.

She directed Paint to his side, the head of her horse facing the back of his. "Love some." She took two long gulps from the canteen he handed her. As she recapped it, she said, "What's that weird-shaped outcrop with grass all around it in the hill back there? I didn't notice it when we rode past it. It must be more obvious from this angle. It doesn't look natural."

Jack looked back over his shoulder. "It's not. My great-grandfather made it. It's the entrance to what's left of the cave with a sod front he built the first winter he lived here. We've kept it as a reminder of what he went through to claim the land grant."

"Someone lived there? Why?"

"The family story is he had to take possession of the land by a certain date and live on it for some specified period of time. He left St. Louis to stake his claim, but it took him longer to get here than he expected. He arrived as winter was setting in and didn't have time to build anything proper. So, he made himself a sod hut that fronted on a shelter he dug out of the hill and lived in it. My great-grandmother stayed back in Missouri with my grandfather and his sisters and came out by wagon train the following spring."

"How did he survive the winter?"

Jack grinned. "Some of *your* ancestors saved his ass. Apparently, the local Indians took pity on him and showed him what to hunt and where to find water. Even gave him food from their stores." He took the canteen from her and hung it on his saddle horn.

"If it hadn't been for your relatives, I wouldn't be here. I'd probably be someplace in Massachusetts where my great-grandparents started out from. I'm quite sure my great-grandmother would never have come west alone."

Quanna was quiet for a moment. "Has anyone from your family told the story to the director of the Tamastslikt museum on the reservation?"

"Don't think so. Why?"

"It's part of the history of the communities both off and on the rez, a good part, not a bad one."

"You tell me who to contact, and I'll dig out my great-grandmother's diaries and let them have a look."

For another hour, they rode leisurely around some of the five hundred acres of the ranch with what must have appeared to Quanna no purpose or goal in mind. But Jack knew exactly where he was headed—a small oasis in the otherwise sunny plain, a pond surrounded by cottonwoods and alders and fed by a small stream that now, in the height of summer, was a slow trickle.

"This is where we winter over the cattle," Jack said. He pointed to a track leading over the nearby hill. "We access it by pickup so we can haul in feed. They have water here. It's sheltered from the worst of the weather. In the summer, we used to play here as kids." He dismounted and put his hand out to help Quanna do the same. "When he was older, my brother would bring his girlfriends here to make out. He doesn't know I know that. I plan to use it someday when his sons do something similar."

"You didn't bring your girlfriends here?"

"Only ever had one and, no. We made out at her parents' ranch."

Jack removed the saddlebag from his horse, and Quanna grabbed the one on hers. The blanket was spread and the pillows laid out, hats and gloves were shed, and the food arranged. Jack had packed whatever he could find in the refrigerator—cold chicken, sliced tomatoes, coleslaw—and had added potato chips, bread, grapes, and a couple apples from the pantry.

"The apples are for ..." he began but stopped when he saw her holding out an apple to Paint. He picked up the other one for Hero.

After they finished eating most of what he'd pulled out of his saddlebag, Quanna stretched out on the blanket and, extending her arms over her head, yawned. "I have to admit, the idea of a nap isn't such a bad idea."

He lay on his side, his head propped up on his bent arm. "Feel free to doze off. I'll keep watch in case we're attacked by hostile bison."

"I don't think there are any bison around here, hostile or otherwise."

"See how good I am at keeping them away?" he said.

She laughed, as he'd hoped she would. Then she turned on her side and faced him, getting serious. "Thank you for this afternoon, Jack. It was wonderful."

He touched her face with the tips of his fingers. "You deserve any treat I can give you. You're one amazing woman." He leaned over and touched his lips to hers. He meant it to be a quick, gentle kiss, but when he began to pull away, she put her arm around his neck, drawing him closer, pressing her mouth to his.

The heat generated by the touch of their lips and her soft moan sent the connection between them into overdrive in seconds. All his restraint disappeared in a kiss that was hot and intense; it laid claim to her, body and soul. He lowered her onto her back and levered over her, his mouth still on hers, his leg insinuated between her thighs. His tongue was demanding entrance to her mouth, and she gave it to him willingly, tangling her tongue with his in a frantic dance. Breathless, he drew back for a second before returning to nip at her lower lip and then taking her mouth again, her hot, sweet, beautiful mouth. Her small sounds of pleasure fueled his desire to keep going, to take it further, to do what he had wanted to do for weeks—make her his.

When he slid his hand inside her shirt, feeling hot skin on hot skin, she shivered, arching toward him as he caressed her breast and tweaked her nipple to a hard point. Her response said she was completely in tune with the kiss and where they both knew it was leading.

Something, maybe the rock he could feel under the blanket close to her, maybe his better judgment, gave him a sudden and unwelcome jolt of mental cold water. He could have rationalized it was time to finally have what he wanted. Could have kept going when it was obvious they both wanted the same thing. But she deserved more than a first time on a blanket on hard, uncomfortable ground.

Now he was the one who groaned. And it wasn't from passion. Slowly, he disentangled his leg from hers, sat up, and carefully rearranged her shirt. When he saw the surprise in her eyes, he tried to think of a way to explain what he'd done that made any sense. But his mind was still muddled from the touch of her mouth, the feel of her skin. He wasn't fast enough to head off her question.

"What's wrong, Jack?"

"I didn't mean to go so far so fast. I should apologize. I don't know what happened."

Her soft laugh startled him. She sounded amused, not upset.

"Should I assume you'll apologize every time you kiss me?"

"You can tell how out of practice I am. You must think I'm an idiot." He pulled at a couple pieces of dried grass peeking out from under the blanket, trying to avoid looking at her.

"First of all, someone who kisses like you do obviously doesn't need much practice to be good. Second, you're kinda cute when you apologize."

That brought his attention back to her. "Cute? Jesus. I think I'd rather have you tell me I'm an idiot."

"I promise I'll keep your secret. But you *are* cute when you tell me you're sorry for kissing me."

He pulled her up so she was sitting, too. "I'll let you get away with calling me cute if you'll let me bumble along and try to explain what happened." He took her hands in his, raised them to his lips, and kissed them. "I want you. More than I've wanted anything in a long time. I want to make love to you. But not here. You deserve better. I shouldn't have kissed you, shouldn't have started anything here. Not when every time I touch you, my brain gets fried and all I can think about is having more of you."

This was it. Time to jump off the cliff or walk away.

"So, here goes. Me maybe making an even bigger fool of myself than I already have. Why don't we ride back to the house and have dessert, maybe a glass of wine, and then, why don't you stay with me tonight?"

· · ·

When she'd answered "I thought you'd never ask" to his question, she'd seen surprise flash across Jack's face before it was replaced with one of his huge grins. He'd packed up the picnic leftovers, the blanket, and pillows so fast she barely had time to brush her jeans off and put the cap back on.

But now, riding back to the house, time seemed to have slowed. Which wasn't good. It gave her too much time to think about what they had started at the picnic site and where it was about to lead. Too much time to get nervous. She'd fantasized about the possibility of this happening from the first month she'd worked at the Richardson Ranch. The only reason she hadn't done anything to make her fantasy come true was she didn't want to risk her job. But it was about to happen. Had she made a mistake?

No, the attraction this man held for her was powerful. Just kissing him turned her into something soft, hot, and needy. Then why was she nervous? A chorus of nasty little voices in her head answered—if it didn't work out, she could lose her job. She could fail her family, have to delay finishing school yet again. One particularly annoying voice insisted she could never satisfy a man like him, a man who was older, with a long and happy marriage behind him. The way he kissed was proof of just what he'd expect.

All the voices in her head had gone hoarse from yelling at her by the time they reached the road to the house. She was grateful to have something to do when they got to the barn so she could ignore them. She immediately unsaddled Paint and began to wipe him down with a towel and curry comb.

"We'll take care of the horses later. I have other things in mind for now," Jack said. He took the towel and comb from her hands and drew her close. "Something like this." He lowered his head and brushed his mouth across hers and pressed her soft body against the hard planes of his muscular one. Being kissed and touched by him raised the temperature of her body more than the sun had. The heat burned out the noises in her head long enough for her to enjoy being expertly kissed.

He used the tip of his tongue to part her lips then slowly, languidly made love to her mouth. At the same time, his hands traveled her soft curves, generating heat with each inch he covered. First her waist, then her hips, snugging her against his erection. She was dizzy with wanting him.

He broke from the kiss. "Shouldn't we take this inside?" His voice was husky and low, his eyes dark with desire.

She choked on her answer. She was beginning to feel like a ping-pong ball, one minute melting with passion, the next listening to the voices in her head telling her to be cautious. She took a step back and picked up the towel again. "We should get Hero and Paint settled. It won't take long."

"I guess I'm happy you care about the horses, but somehow my gratitude level is a bit low at the moment." He picked up another towel and, with a half smile, went to wipe down his horse.

Once the horses were cooled down, watered, fed, and stabled, she couldn't avoid the inevitable. He took her hand as they left the barn, but when they got into the house, she dropped his hand and moved to put the breakfast island between them. He cocked his head and looked as if he had a question for her, but when he spoke, it wasn't the one she expected. "How 'bout that dessert or a glass of wine?"

"No, thanks." She shook her head. "I'm so sweaty and horsey smelling, I'm not sure I'm a fit eating or drinking companion."

"Well, you know where the shower is and how to find towels. Be my guest."

His immediate response surprised her. "Okay. If it's all right with you, I will take a shower."

She couldn't see his face as he grabbed a bottle of beer from the refrigerator and twisted off the cap. He took a swig without turning around. "Showering sounds good, now that I think about it."

"I'll leave enough hot water for you, I promise."

"Or ..." He hesitated for a moment, then faced her. "I could join you. The shower's big enough for two."

There was such hunger in his eyes. Her desire for him flared as she saw how much he wanted her. And she surely wanted him. She shut down the voices in her head. If he was willing to take a chance, so was she. "Yes, it is, isn't it?"

"I'll lock up down here and join you in a few minutes." His smile melted the last of her doubts and kept her feeling warm as she ran up the stairs.

•••

Through the steamed up glass walls of the oversized shower enclosure, he could see her silhouette. She appeared to be soaping herself up. He watched for a few moments, his fingers clenching and unclenching, wanting his to be the hands gliding over her body. Needing to touch her.

He slid the door open. She gasped, as if startled by his appearance, and stood still, hands on her breasts, soap dripping down her stomach until the suds were lost in a forest of dark hair at the junction of her thighs. His breath quickened and his cock hardened.

He swept his gaze up and down her body again and groaned as he saw water rinse away the soapsuds so every inch of her coppery brown skin was on display, wet and glistening. "My God. Maybe this isn't such a good idea."

She turned her back to him before saying, "If you've changed your mind about my staying …"

Hands on her shoulders, he gently moved her so she faced him again. Her eyes were shiny, and a crease had appeared between them. "Hell, no, I haven't changed my mind. I meant it was a bad idea to join you in the shower. If it was stupid to roll around with you on a blanket fully clothed, being naked with you right now might be an even worse idea. All I can think of is how easy it would be to pick you up, press you against the wall, and take you." He pulled her arms up so they were around his neck and kissed her forehead.

She sniffed, and a small, tremulous smile tried to appear. "I'm getting your shirt wet."

"Then I guess I better take it off." He stepped back, and stripped off his shirt, jeans, and boxer briefs in seconds before walking into the shower.

"I thought you said it was a bad idea."

He took the washcloth she was holding and, drawing her back against his chest, began to caress her breasts and belly with it. "I'm seriously reconsidering that statement."

As he continued to massage her breasts, he nuzzled her neck. Her back arched; her nipples tightened. "Finished reconsidering. I was definitely wrong. This is a very good idea." His erection pressed into her, causing her to moan.

He nipped his way from her shoulder to her ear. "I knew you were damn beautiful," he whispered. "But my imagination didn't do you justice. Your skin is so soft and smooth. You taste so good."

He dropped the washcloth, and holding her against him with one arm, he slipped the other one over her stomach and down to her sex. She canted her hips forward to give him access as he massaged gently, all the while kissing her neck, her shoulder, her ear.

From the pace of her breathing and the beating of her heart—which was keeping time with his—she was as aroused as he was. He knew if they didn't stop, their first time would be quick, soon, and very, very wet.

"We need to get out of here." Reaching around her, he turned off the water, then opened the door and stepped out. He offered his hand to her so she could follow.

When they were both wrapped in towels, he scooped her up into his arms and started toward the bedroom.

She nestled into him, and he could feel her smile against his neck. "Showing off?"

"Nope. This is the fastest way to get you to my bed."

Chapter 12

In the shower, Jack had been sure she'd been as ready for this as he was, but when they got to his bed and he unwrapped her from her towel, the desire in her eyes had dimmed. She seemed nervous, scared even.

"Are you okay? You look ... I don't know ... uneasy, maybe."

She dropped onto the bed, avoiding his eyes. "No, I'm fine." She shook her head. "Okay, maybe a little nervous. It's been a while for me since ... you know."

He took her chin in his hand and tipped her face up. "Me, too. So we'll take it nice and easy. Make sure we're both happy with what we're doing."

"Okay." She looked less nervous, but doubt was still apparent on her face.

"First thing to make me happy is you have to scoot over. You're on my side of the bed, and I'm a creature of habit."

She scooted. And laughed.

He dropped the towel from around his hips and saw the approving look in her eyes as her gaze swept up and down his body. It certainly helped his confidence that she seemed to appreciate what she saw.

Settling on his side facing her, he ran his hand over the curves he'd wanted to touch for weeks, hoping he was reassuring her, not reminding her of how he gentled Hero when the horse got frisky. When she still seemed tense, he made another suggestion. "There's another thing that would make me happy. Something I've wanted to do for a long time."

"What's that?" The uneasiness was still there in her voice.

He reached behind her and moved her braid over her shoulder. "I want to see if your hair feels as silky as it looks. Can I undo this?"

She sighed, with relief he thought, and nodded.

He removed the band holding the strands of the braid together and began to untangle it. She shook her head, and the braid came loose, almost in slow motion, draping over her shoulder just as he imagined it would.

"Damn, it really is like silk. I could spend hours doing this," he said as he forked his fingers through the long strands of coal black hair. "But that's two for me and none for you. It's your turn. What would make you happy?"

"I'm not sure I know how to answer." The crease between her eyes that always meant she was wary appeared as she continued. "What, exactly, do you mean?"

He nipped at her shoulder and drew closer to her, feeling the warmth of her skin on his belly and legs. "What do you like when you make love? What gives you pleasure?"

"I ... I guess I've never thought about it."

"Are you challenging me to find out on my own?" The crease between her eyes deepened so he quickly added. "I'm not objecting. I like the challenge of exploring." He took her chin in one hand. "I think I'll start here ..."

He captured her lips with his. He didn't bother with soft, sweet preliminaries this time but went straight for owning her lips, her tongue, hell, he'd have tried for her soul if he could have reached it with his mouth.

When he drew back, he could see the concern in her eyes had been replaced with clouds of desire. "That's better. Now let's see what else you like," he said and began a slow, sensuous slide with his mouth from her cheek to her jaw, then to her neck, resting at the pulse in her throat before nibbling his way to her breasts and the dusky nipples there. This time it was his mouth, not his fingers, that brought her nipples to diamond hard peaks, first one then the other. When she breathed out "yes" and grabbed his arms as if afraid he would stop—as if he would, as if he could—he knew he'd found another sweet spot. And he knew there were more to be discovered.

Only now, he was the one with a problem—he wasn't sure he could stick to his promise to take it nice and easy. He could feel the pressure building in his body, the need in his mind, to finally, once and for all, have all of her. He didn't want to rush her, but he was more than ready. Had been for days, weeks maybe.

His erection could have broken bricks, he was sure, but he gritted his teeth, took a deep breath, and returned his attention to her mouth. Her hands were in his hair, and she was making soft, urgent sounds in the back of her throat as he kissed her. She ground her hips against him, one leg now over his hip. He felt her wetness on his thigh. Thank God, she was aroused, too.

Turning her onto her back, he slid his hand between her thighs and found the nub of her clitoris. He began to gently, slowly massage it. "Tell me how this feels, baby."

When she didn't answer for a moment, he wondered if he'd lost his touch from lack of practice. But then on a long, slow exhale, she answered, "Oh, God, that feels so good."

Her hands gripped the sheet under them as he thrust one finger, then another, deep into her. His thumb continued to circle her clitoris, his fingers massaging inside her. It took only a few seconds before her internal muscles clenched around his fingers, and she gasped and rocked her hips up at him. It was all he could do to keep from substituting his penis for his fingers, pounding into her, releasing his passion as he was releasing hers. But he didn't. He waited for her to come down from her orgasm, to say something, before he continued.

Instead she was still and silent. He gathered her into his arms. "You okay, sweetheart?" Her body was covered in a sheen of sweat; her breathing was shallow and rapid; her eyes were unfocused.

It took a few moments before she answered. "No, I'm not okay. I'm wonderful. *You're* wonderful."

The relief he felt was incalculable.

"We're only getting started," he promised.

• • •

What else would match the way he'd made her feel? She'd just had the most amazing physical experience of her life. It was like nothing she'd ever known before. Other than his chance to have the same feeling, what was left?

"Time for more exploring, don't you think?" he whispered. When he traced the edge of her ear with the tip of his tongue, she shivered with desire. Again. Apparently he was about to show her what else there was.

He captured one of her breasts with his mouth. The nipple, sensitized from his previous ministrations, reacted immediately, sending jolts of ecstasy through her. He moved back to her mouth and as soon as his tongue touched her lips, she opened for him, eagerly taking him in. She grasped his biceps and pulled him closer to her.

Abruptly, he moved back from her. She wanted to hold on to him, to keep him close. She couldn't figure out why he was leaving her. But he wasn't leaving. He was putting on a condom. The thought flickered through her head that he had prepared carefully for this evening.

He moved slowly down her body with his mouth. His hands stayed on her waist while he tasted, sucked, and licked under her breasts, then down to her navel, then ever so carefully to the place between her thighs where he found her clitoris, still aroused from the first orgasm, and paid the same attention to it he had to her breasts.

Unbelievably, she felt another climax begin deep inside her. It was so intense, grew so fast, felt so powerful she was barely able to breathe. As she was about to crest the wave, she felt him enter her with only the head of his penis.

"Tell me how it feels, baby. Tell me what you want." His voice was thick and hoarse.

"More, I want more of you." She wanted to be filled with him, in a way no man had ever filled her before. With her legs around his hips and her arms around his body, she pulled at him so he would fully enter her. She moaned with pleasure. "Oh, yes. That's what I want."

She expected him to satisfy himself now, but he surprised her by shifting his body in some way so there was still pressure on her clitoris as he thrust within her. Her second orgasm continued to increase in strength until it finally crashed over her like a tsunami. Only as she was coming down from the most earth-shattering climax of her life did he reach his release and collapse in her arms.

For a few moments, the only sounds in the room were of two people trying to calm their breathing and regain their footing on the shifting sands of this new phase of their relationship. A relationship that Quanna knew could have consequences she was still unsure of but which, after their amazing lovemaking, was already more important than it should be. She'd known, after the way he'd defended her from the bullies in the bar and from her nasty neighbor, that he was a kind, decent man. That he was also a tender, thoughtful, and very thorough lover shouldn't have surprised her. But it did. It also moved her in ways she hadn't expected. Moved her to the brink of tears.

Finally, he pushed himself up and went to the bathroom to take care of the condom. When he returned, he slid back under the sheet and held her silently for a while. Then something made him look carefully at her face.

She knew what it was and tried to hide, but he was too close to miss it.

"Oh, hell. You're crying. I hurt you." He wiped away the tear hanging on the edge of her eyelid. "I'm sorry, sweetheart. Tell me what I did, and I won't do it again."

"You didn't hurt me. I'm not sad crying. I'm ... I don't know ... emotional crying, I guess." She tried to pull away from him, but he wouldn't let her go.

"Why? Tell me. Please."

"Making love with you was ... I don't even know the word to use. It was amazing. Incredible. I didn't know it could be so good." She stroked his face, gave him a quick kiss. "It's like I've never really known what sex was until now."

"It was pretty amazing for me, too." He was playing with her hair again, combing his fingers through it.

She buried her face in his shoulder so he couldn't see her as she went on. "No one's ever cared ... ever asked me what I liked ... what I wanted. Never made sure ..." She stopped. Almost afraid to go on, to admit what had happened to make her so emotional. But she owed him the truth. "Never made sure I was, what did you say we'd be? Happy? Anyway, I've never had ... never been able to come during sex with a partner. Only by myself. Not until tonight."

His hand froze in her hair. He slumped back on the pillow, snorting. "Huh. I'll be damned."

She untangled herself from his hand and moved a few inches toward the side of the bed. She had opened herself up to him, and he'd laughed. How could he? "I'm glad it amuses you."

He was quick to pull her back into his arms even though she struggled to keep a distance between them. "I wasn't laughing. It's just that I spent hours today, I swear, worrying about whether I'd disappoint you in bed, assuming I ever got you here. I'd have been a lot less distracted if I'd known what you just told me." He kissed her on the forehead. "I'm sorry. I didn't mean to hurt your feelings."

"*You* were worried? Why?"

"Like I said, it's been a while and I'm a lot older. Plus, I've only been with one woman. I figured I might not be up to your standard."

"My standard, if you can call it that, is a high school boyfriend who was as inexperienced as I was and a boyfriend in Portland who thought all I needed to do to have a good time was loosen up with a lot of wine before we went to bed. The truth is, I was worried I wouldn't live up to your expectations. I figured, with all the time you had with one woman, you'd be good, and I wasn't sure I could keep up."

"The part about you not keeping up isn't true. You more than keep up. You turn me inside out." He grinned and she touched his dimples, like she'd always wanted to.

She smiled back at him. "So tell me, is it experience that makes you so amazing or are you naturally good in bed?"

"Is anyone 'naturally good in bed'? I was like your high school boyfriend, I imagine, when Paula and I were first together. Over the years, we learned how to give each other pleasure."

"She was a lucky woman to have you to learn with."

The grin reappeared. "Is this what pillow talk is these days—discussions about former bed partners right after sex?"

"Actually, it's supposed to take place before the sex, not after. You know, to find out about STDs."

"Since we established that neither of us had been with anyone for a long time, I think we sorta covered the subject, didn't we?"

"Not necessarily. But I was tested regularly at Golden Years so I'm sure I'm ..." She tried to stifle it, but a yawn overtook her.

"You're about to fall asleep, aren't you? It's been a long day. We can finish this conversation in the morning." He spooned around her, kissed her shoulder, and pulled the sheet up over both of them. "Sleep well, sweetheart."

Chapter 13

Quanna woke to an empty bed. She wasn't sure how long Jack had been gone. She thought she remembered him slipping away sometime in the night, but she couldn't recall hearing him return. Now she wondered if he had gone into another room, maybe because he wasn't used to sleeping with anyone in his bed. Or she snored. She didn't want to think it was something else. Like regrets.

She slid out of bed and put on her panties and shirt. It took only a few minutes to establish he wasn't in any of the rooms on the second floor. Barefoot, she padded down the steps listening for sounds of someone else in the house, but there were none. There was definitely the aroma of coffee so she knew he had made it to the kitchen at some point.

He was still there. As she crossed the living room, she could see him sitting at the breakfast bar, his favorite mug in front of him, head bent, staring down at the counter, his hands on his forehead. She got to the doorway without his hearing her.

"You look like a man who's having morning-after second thoughts." His head jerked up. He didn't smile as he usually did when he saw her. She tried to sound upbeat and positive even though her heart was breaking. "It's okay. I understand. I'll leave as soon as I get dressed and we'll rewind to last week before any of this happened." She wasn't sure how she planned to do that but if she wanted to retain any of her sanity, much less her job, she'd have to. She'd start figuring it out as soon as she left for home. Which she better do quickly before she made her tears last night look like nothing. She spun on her heel and took two steps toward the stairs.

"Regrets? Leave? What are you talking about?"

She didn't want him to see how hurt she was so she didn't turn around to face him. "It's obvious, isn't it? You were so eager to get away from me you left your own bed in the middle of the night. And right now you look like a man who's miserable. Not like someone who ..."

"Made love to a beautiful woman last night?"

She felt his presence behind her even before he touched her. "I don't want you to leave, sweetheart. Unless you want to." He turned her and wrapped his arms around her. "Do you want to?"

"No, I don't. But I'll go if you don't want me here."

"I want you here. Believe me, I want you." He rested his cheek on her head, and she could feel the vibration of his deep voice as he said, "I didn't desert you in the middle of the night. I woke up at five like I always do. I watched you sleep for a bit—you looked so peaceful. You needed sleep so I didn't want to wake you. But I knew if I stayed, I'd pounce on you like a hawk on a sage grouse so I left to get away from the temptation."

She looked up at him, sure the relief she was feeling must show on her face. "The explanation was working until it got to the part where I'm a sage grouse."

He didn't laugh, didn't even smile. "Well, I didn't like it either but probably not for the same reason. It got me thinking. Was I a predator, too, like the hawks we saw yesterday? I've been sitting here trying to decide."

"A predator? Why?"

He took her hand, led her to the couch in the living room, and settled her with her head on his shoulder. Stroking her arm, he continued. "A predator takes advantage of someone who's vulnerable. Is that what I'm doing? You depend on your job here, hell, your family depends on your job here. Maybe you felt you couldn't say 'no.' I mean ..."

She didn't know if she was more relieved or amused by his explanation. It was apparent he wasn't having regrets; he was merely being the man he was. Amusement won. And a little fake righteous indignation. "You think I slept with you to keep my job? What kind of woman do you think I am, Jack?"

"I didn't say that. Or at least, I didn't mean that."

"Sure sounded like it to me." She sat up, trying to look as stern as she could. "Listen carefully to me, Jack Richardson, because I'm only saying this once. If the subject ever, and I mean ever, comes up again, I'm out of here faster than you can say—oh, I don't know, some short word." She wagged her finger at him when she thought he was about to laugh.

"If anyone is a predator," she continued, "it's me. Hitting on a vulnerable, lonely widower whose only company is his horse and his kids." She couldn't stop him from laughing this time. "Seriously, I've come close to quitting my job here because I wanted to see if I could get you to look at me as a woman and not your kid wrangler. The only reason I didn't is I didn't want to fail my family. Well, and I fell in love with your boys and couldn't bear the thought of leaving them."

"For God's sake, don't quit. My kids would kill me." He kissed her softly. "And forgive me for what I said. I should have warned you how bad I am at figuring out romantic relationships. I'd do better if you were livestock or wheat. Those I can figure out."

"All of a sudden, sage grouse doesn't sound so bad." She wound her arms around his neck. "But if we're finished comparing me to various forms of animal and plant life, could we go back to bed?"

"I was waiting for you to wake up so I could make you breakfast." He stood and held out his hand to help her up.

"Later. I thought I might get you to give me more of the benefit of your years of experience learning how to give a woman pleasure."

"That, sweetheart, I'm more than willing to do."

• • •

"So, what's on your 'to do' list today?" Quanna was clearing the breakfast bar after the pancakes Jack had fixed for them.

"Nothing fun. I have some chores to get done. Then maybe we can watch a movie. I should have told you to bring something to entertain yourself while I'm mucking out the stables."

"Movie sounds great. But let me help with the mucking. I'm good at it. After all, I muck out Lucas's room on a regular basis."

"Thank God you do. Otherwise we'd lose him in the mess he makes every day." He took the dishes from her and began to load the dishwasher. "I appreciate the offer, but if I let you wallow around in horseshit as part of our first weekend together, it would cement my reputation as the least romantic man in the state."

She hip-bumped him out of the way. "You cooked. I clean up." She changed the arrangement of the dishes as she continued. "You should worry more about my ratting you out about how cute you are when you apologize for kissing me."

He grabbed her and pulled her toward him. "Since I've already earned the humiliation, I might as well give you another example to back it up. This time I'll apologize in advance." He took her chin in his hand. "I'm sorry for distracting you from your chore, sweetheart, but it's been too long since the last time I did this." She was smiling when he kissed her.

Quanna won. She helped muck out the stable. Fresh hay was spread, with the totally predictable suggestion they have a roll in it. Horses were fed and watered. After another shower, during which he did press her to the wall and make love to her, they watched *Iron Man*, which Quanna admitted she kinda liked. Until he told her there were two more they could watch if she was really interested. She confessed she hadn't liked it that much.

When Jack began to make noises about dinner, Quanna said, "I think I should go home after we eat. I don't want to wear out my welcome."

"As if you could." He dropped a kiss on the top of her head. "Why don't you stay here for the rest of the week until the boys come home? And maybe drive to Portland with me to pick them up."

"I can't stay here all week. I'm working the breakfast shift at the resort Monday, Wednesday, and Friday. The ranch is far enough away from the reservation that I'd have to get up even earlier than you do to get there by six forty-five."

"All right. Then, how about we plan things so I'll see you every day. Tuesday and Thursday you'll be here and can stay for dinner with me. What do you want to do on the other days?"

"I still think you are trying to fatten me up."

"If you don't want to have dinner, what would you like to do?"

"A movie at the theater at the resort? Maybe another horseback ride? What do you like to do for fun?"

"Right now, reading a book when the kids are in bed or watching some mindless TV show is as exciting as it gets. I'm a real ball of fire."

"Actually, a quiet evening reading a good book would be a treat for me, too. Most of what I read is for class."

"I don't think I know the answer to this—are you taking a class now?"

"No. I took the summer off. I'll make up for it with two classes fall term."

"So all I have to compete with is your other job. If you won't stay, can I at least see you every day? In addition to work, I mean."

"I guess we can make that happen." She hoped her grin told him it was more than a guess.

"Then you can drive to Portland with me to get the boys. On the way back, we can tell them about us and ..."

"No! We can't."

"Why not? Are you saying after next weekend we'll go back to our old relationship, and I'll only see you in passing when you're here to work?"

"Yes. I mean, no. I didn't mean we'd go back to the way things were before this week." She took his hand. "Look, Jack, we don't know what this last week has been about, do we? It could just be a fling or …"

"I don't do flings."

"Okay, but you're missing the point." She put her hand up to wave off what she was sure was about to be another objection. "What would we tell them? How would we describe it? We're sleeping together? We're friends with benefits? What?"

"Why can't we say we're dating?"

"It could upset them."

"Or they could love it."

"Which might be even worse. We don't know where this is going. The boys could have expectations that could mess up my relationship with them."

"I don't like lying to my sons."

"You're not lying. You're omitting a few details about what you did while they were gone."

"So, a sin of omission rather than commission? That's not much better. And what about when they're back home and I want to see you? Or are you saying we won't be with each other after this week? Other than while you're working, I mean."

"No, we'll have to figure it out. Find a way. I'm not suggesting it'll be easy." She squeezed his hand. "You know I'm right about not telling them now. You don't want them confused or upset, do you? I sure don't. I care for them too much."

He sighed. "I hate it. But I guess you're right." He brought their entwined hands up to his lips and kissed her fingertips. "Which makes it even more important for us to be together any bit of time we can this week. So, I'll amend my original question—why don't you stay tonight?"

"I'd love to."

• • •

"Good morning, beautiful."

Jack had watched Quanna sleep for more than an hour after he woke on Sunday morning, feeling the warmth of her body close to him, hearing the regularity of her measured, sleep-shallow breathing. She was as lovely asleep as she was awake. After a while, he couldn't resist touching her, stroking her shoulder, enjoying the softness of her skin. Which had led to a definite increase in the hardness of his erection.

He wasn't sure if he moved or made a sound. Maybe she sensed his arousal. Whatever it was, she stirred, yawned, and stretched. "Mmm. What time is it?"

"It's a little past six."

"And you're still in bed? How come?"

"Either I didn't want to panic you two days in a row about where I was or you look less like a sage grouse today. You pick."

She linked her arms around his neck. "That's not the way to get lucky before breakfast, Jack."

"Then let's try this." He kissed his way from her ear to her neck while he caressed her breast. Turned out, that was the way.

An hour later, both had showered and Jack had gone downstairs to put coffee on, wearing only a pair of jeans. Because he'd insisted on washing her hair, mostly so he had an excuse to play with it, Quanna stayed upstairs to get it dried.

He had the coffee dripping and was examining the contents of the refrigerator to see what he wanted to make for their breakfast when he heard the front door open and a familiar woman's voice call out. "Jack? Are you in the kitchen?"

It was his sister Barbara.

"There you are," she said as she kissed his cheek. "I'm glad I caught you. I was afraid you'd be off someplace already. But obviously you haven't eaten yet. And you're humming. Must be a good morning."

Damn. He hadn't realized he was making any noise at all, let alone humming. "What're you doing out so early on a Sunday morning, Barb?" If she noticed his furtive look over her shoulder, hoping he wouldn't see Quanna coming downstairs, she didn't act like it. The conversation with Quanna about figuring out what was going on between them before they tried to explain it to other people now made sense. How the hell would he explain his nanny being there to his sister?

"I decided to drop in on my big brother because he's been all alone for a week and I was afraid he might be getting lonely. And I know how early you get up. So, here I am at the crack of dawn. At least it is for me." She settled herself at the end of the breakfast bar. "How about pouring me a cup of that coffee I smell. Then you can tell me how you got on this week all by your lonesome."

He filled a mug for her. "I'm fine. Got a lot done. After two weeks with four boys here, I had a bunch to catch up on."

"I'm glad you restarted the tradition with Sam's boys. They loved being here. I sure enjoyed having them over at our place. Though when all of our kids are together, they're a handful. Thank heaven for Quanna. She's amazing. You were lucky to find her."

"Yeah, I know." *You have no idea how lucky.*

"When are you retrieving them? When they get back, I'd like to squeeze in one more camping trip if we can before school starts."

"I drive over next Sunday, come home on Monday. Another campout would be fine, but we start harvest as soon as I'm back and ..."

Paying attention to his conversation with his sister, he missed the fact that Quanna had come downstairs. He only heard her when she was two steps away from walking into the kitchen. She was barefoot, dressed in his shirt with God-knows-what underneath, and her unbraided hair looked slightly damp. She might as well have had a sign around her neck saying, "I spent the night."

He didn't have a chance to warn her before she saw who was sitting at the island and screeched to a halt in the doorway. "Oh. Ah ... hi, Barbara. I didn't know you were here," she said, her voice squeaking a bit at the end of the sentence.

Barbara raised an eyebrow at Jack before she said, "Hello, Quanna. I didn't know you were here either."

"I'm ... ah ... I was just ... ah ... I mean ... I came to get coffee, and then I'll ... I guess I'll go finish what I was doing upstairs." She dropped her gaze, scurried to the coffeepot, filled a mug, and looked like she was about to head for the stairs.

As his mother used to say, might as well be hung for a sheep as a lamb. He put his arm around her shoulder, kissed the top of her head, and said, "I'll join you in a few minutes. Barb isn't staying long."

He watched his sister's face as Quanna blushed and almost ran out of the room.

"Well," Barbara said after a few moments of awkward silence. "At least now I understand the humming."

"Look, Barb ..."

She waved off his attempt to explain. "I don't need an explanation. But I will ask if you're sure you know what you're doing."

His younger siblings had never questioned his judgment. Not about how he chose to keep the family together after their parents' death. Or what he did to keep the ranch from bankruptcy soon after. Not his choice of crops, cattle breeds, or the color of the paint on the walls of the house that belonged to all three of them. It stung to hear his sister start now.

Which was probably the reason his voice had an edge to it when he answered her question. "I know exactly what I'm doing. Something I haven't done for a long time—living a little bit for myself. Everyone, you included, told me I needed to get back to enjoying life, and I'm finally taking your advice. Not only is Quanna the first woman I've been attracted to in years, but for some odd reason, she returns the feeling. I'll be damned if I'm going to let this chance pass me by."

"Don't be so defensive. I wasn't being critical. It's a bit complicated, don't you think, with her being your nanny and all? I mean, she's young. She's vulnerable. She's your employee. I don't want to see you hurt her."

"You don't have to protect ... wait, you don't want to see *her* hurt?"

"Right. Pain from you is the last thing she deserves. Considering how much she's come to mean to my nephews, I don't want to see their relationship screwed up because you two get involved only to have it go sour."

"We've talked about all that. We're not going to tell anyone, especially the boys, what's going on until we figure it out ourselves. Which won't be easy to do once Daniel and Lucas are home. But I want to try. I care about her. A lot. I want this to work."

Barbara finished off her coffee. "Then I guess I better leave you alone. You only have the week ahead before you have to begin to juggle your kids with your love life—or is it your sex life?"

"Not that it's any of your business, but like I said, we're trying to figure it out ourselves."

She slipped off the stool and came around to where her brother stood. "Seriously, Jack, I'm glad you're finally doing something for yourself. And if I can help, let me know. I can always entertain your sons if you want to slip away for dinner or a movie." She patted him on the shoulder. "I apologize for breaking into your weekend. I promise I won't use my key to come in unannounced again."

He leaned down and kissed his sister's forehead. "You're a good sister. I don't care what Sam says."

She swatted him on the arm. "Funny, he says the same thing only with you as the one who badmouths me. Now, walk me to my car."

She'd started the engine when Jack threw out the question he was almost afraid to ask. "Barb, it doesn't bother you because she's Indian, does it?"

"Now, why the devil would you think it would?"

"Quanna's had nasty comments about her parentage from her neighbor and a few other people, and she's sensitive about it. I told her it wouldn't matter to anyone I knew, but I thought I'd check."

"Of course it doesn't matter." She put the car in gear and started to back out. Then stopped and stuck her head out the window. "Now ask me if I'm concerned because she's a lot younger than you are."

"Okay. Are you?"

"Other than not wanting to see you be the butt of jokes about middle-aged men who fall for younger women, not really. I'll merely say, be prepared for it."

Chapter 14

When he came back into the house, Quanna was sitting on the couch in the living room fully dressed. If her bleak expression was anything like the one she'd seen on his face the morning before, it was no wonder she'd been convinced he was having second thoughts. He hoped to hell she wasn't going to run off at this first glitch in their plan to keep things under wraps.

"She's mad, isn't she, about us being together?"

"No, she isn't. She apologized for breaking into our weekend." He sat next to her and drew her into an embrace. She was trembling. "It's okay, sweetheart. I told her we want to keep things quiet for a while. She won't say anything until we tell her it's okay."

"She didn't warn you away from me?"

"We-e-e-l-l." He dragged out the word hoping to lighten the conversation. It didn't. "She did warn me about one thing. She told me not to hurt you. Didn't quite threaten me, but came close."

"Oh. Why would she do that?"

"She likes you. She also likes the relationship you have with her nephews. She says I'm lucky to have found you." He kissed her forehead. "She's right."

"She didn't try to convince you people will talk because ..."

"Because I'm a middle-aged man and you're a sweet, young thing? Yeah, she mentioned it. But she said she was willing to let it go as long as I was prepared for the gossip."

"I'm not a sweet, young thing, and that's not what I meant. You know what I meant."

"Quanna, sweetheart, I keep telling you, none of my family or friends would ever think your being part Indian would make a difference. It isn't who they are."

"And you've discussed this, have you, with your family and friends?"

"No, not in so many words. But I know them. That kind of prejudice is in the past."

"I wish you were right. You'd be surprised where it comes out, Jack."

After another quick kiss, he stood up. "I guess I'll just have to wait for you to see I know what I'm talking about when we tell people about us. For now, can we please eat? I'm starving. I was about to start breakfast when Barb arrived."

"If you're sure she's not angry about you hooking up with me."

She started to hop up off the couch, but he caught her by the arm. "Don't say that. This wasn't hooking up."

"I'm sorry. I know this isn't a hookup. I don't do hookups."

"So, at least we know two things about what's going on: it's not a fling because I don't do flings. And it's not a hookup because you don't do hookups. If Sherlock's right, all we have to do is eliminate all the wrong answers and whatever we're left with is the truth."

This time, she did laugh. "Makes as much sense as anything does." She caught him by the belt loop on his jeans as he started back to the kitchen. "Let me cook this morning. You put some music on."

• • •

As she cracked eggs and chopped veggies for omelets, the sound of piano music drifted in from the living room. She thought she'd heard the piece before, but she couldn't put a title to it.

She was still trying to figure out if she knew what the music was when the pianist hit the wrong key. It seemed odd such a mistake made it to a recording. She stopped to listen more closely and heard a second discordant note.

Curious, she returned to the living room where she saw Jack at the piano. He was playing for her.

"I think I've heard that music before, but I don't know the name of it," she said as he made room for her to join him on the piano bench.

"It's Beethoven. 'Fur Elise.' Piano student standard. But I'm having trouble remembering it. Or maybe, more accurately, playing it." He started to put the cover back over the keyboard.

"Don't. Please keep going. Unless playing brings back bad memories."

"No, only good ones. We each practiced with my mother for half an hour after school every day. I wasn't crazy about it at the time, but now I realize how much it meant to me to have her undivided attention for that half hour."

"It meant a lot to her, too, I imagine."

"She was headed for a career as a concert pianist when she came to Oregon to visit an uncle, met my dad, fell in love, and stayed. She never regretted her decision, she said. But sometimes I wonder. She would have loved knowing how much Paula played, even as an adult. No one's touched the damn piano since she died."

"You haven't arranged lessons for the boys, have you? Both your mother and theirs would want them to learn, don't you think?"

"Yeah, they would." He noodled around, playing several scale progressions.

"Maybe once school starts, I can find someone ... we can find ... uh, you can find someone to teach them. I'd be glad to ferry them to lessons, if that's what it takes."

He slid closer to her on the piano bench and crooked his index finger under her chin. "I like the way it sounds when you say 'we' can do something with the boys."

"I don't mean to try to tell you how to raise your sons."

"You're not. You're helping raise them." He kissed her. "We better get breakfast going before I start to get ideas about what can be done on a piano bench other than play the piano."

• • •

In spite of Quanna's shifts at the restaurant, Jack's long days in the fields, and her determination to make her time at the ranch only work, they found time to fit in a movie, a couple dinners, and another horseback ride during the following week. They spent a few more nights together, made love when the mood hit them, which it did with some frequency, and began to learn about each other in ways more intimate than just boss and kid wrangler.

Quanna reminded herself at least once a day it might not last forever. And warned herself that if it didn't, she might not be able to work for him. At least, she didn't think she could. But if she had to leave the Richardson Ranch, she'd be right back where she'd been in the spring trying to find enough money to meet her obligation to her family, finish college, and pay her rent. Then there was the other problem, the one Jack didn't like to talk about. In spite of what he thought, she was sure he'd have family or friends who would never accept her as worthy of him. Being with her could hurt his reputation or give bullies an excuse to harass the boys. She couldn't let that happen.

In spite of all her self-talk, after spending the second Friday and Saturday night at the ranch, she drove back to her apartment on Sunday morning to wait for Jack to call when he got to Portland, knowing the truth. She had fallen for the man. Hard. She also knew it was possible that it all could fall apart, and all she would ever have was two weeks of being loved by Jack Richardson. That might have to be enough even if she wanted more.

• • •

"Hey, sweetheart. Sorry to call so late." Jack kept his voice low so he wouldn't be overheard.

"You got to Portland okay. That's all that matters. Were the boys happy to see you?"

"For about fifteen minutes. Then they headed down to the basement with their cousins to finish up some video game or another." He looked over his shoulder to make sure he was still alone. "I had to wait until after dinner and the kids were all being settled in bed before I could sneak out on the deck and call you. I miss you."

"I miss you, too. I hope you don't mind. I brought home one of your shirts to sleep in. I'll return it on Monday."

He groaned. "You're killing me. I have to sleep alone in a strange bed tonight. I should have brought something of yours with me for company."

"You'd look silly trying to wear one of my T-shirts, but I like the idea. When will you be home tomorrow?"

"We'll leave in time to be back by dinner. Will you be there?"

"I won't leave until you get here. I want to see Daniel and Lucas."

"Only my sons?"

"And you." She laughed. He was always happy to be the cause of that sound.

"Because I definitely want to see you," he responded.

Their conversation was interrupted by a discrete cough from behind him. Jack did a 180 and saw Sam standing in the doorway leading into the house, a smirk on his face.

"All of a sudden, I'm not alone. I better go. I'll see you tomorrow."

"Safe trip home."

He ended the call, jammed the phone into his jeans pocket, and waited for what he was sure would be a cross-examination. It didn't take long.

"So," Sam started. "I hear you had quite a weekend last week. Did you spend *any* time by yourself while the boys were here?"

"How would you know about my weekend?"

"Our beloved sister." He made a mock surprise face. "You thought she would keep it to herself? How long have you known her?"

"Jesus, after I asked her to keep quiet about it, she called you?"

"Of course she did. It made my day. I've been waiting since I was a teenager for you to come down off your pedestal and join us here on earth. And to make it even better, it happened because you're twisted in knots about a woman just like the rest of us mortal men. I can die happy."

"I'd be glad to help you reach your goal—the dying part, I mean."

"No, you wouldn't. Who'd give you advice about your love life if I wasn't here?"

"I can manage my own love life, thanks."

"So it *is* 'love life' and not 'sex life.' Barb wasn't sure."

"Fuck you, Sam. I'm not one of your suspects. I don't have to put up with your cop interrogation tricks." He tried to push past his brother to get back in the house, but Sam wouldn't let him pass.

"Seriously, Jack, I'm happy for you. When were you going to tell me?"

"I wasn't planning on telling anyone until we've decided where the relationship's going. It was an accident Barb found out."

"So she said." He started to open the sliding screen door. "If you won't give me details, can I at least get a hint where you *want* the relationship to go?"

Jack looked Sam straight in the eyes and said, "As far as she'll go with me."

Sam slung an arm around his brother's shoulders and pushed open the door the rest of the way. "Then I hope it works out for you."

. . .

Quanna had been waiting for an hour in the living room trying—and failing—to read. No matter how hard she'd tried to concentrate on her book, all she'd been able to think about was how it would play out when Jack and the boys arrived home. Would she and Jack go back to the friendly but professional relationship they'd had before? Or would they have a hard time hiding what had happened over the past two weeks? Would the boys notice something was different? How would Jack handle it if his sons asked questions?

When she heard the crunch of gravel signaling the arrival of Jack's truck, her heartbeat kicked up in anticipation. The front door banged open, and Lucas came running in, throwing his arms around her as soon as she stood and before she could even say hello.

"Quanna!" he said. "You're here."

She kissed the top of his head. "I didn't want to wait until tomorrow to see you. I hear you had a great time in Portland."

"It was awesome. We went to the beach and the zoo. We heard a concert in a park. We went on the alpine slide on Mt. Hood. Uncle Sam took us to work with him, and we got to sit in a real police car."

"You had a good time, too, Daniel?" She extended her arm to him, and he let her hug him, too.

"Yeah, it was great hanging out with Sammy and Jack at Uncle Sam's. They have cool video games." Daniel wasn't quite so demonstrative, but it was obvious from his face he'd enjoyed the vacation.

"I'm glad you're home. I missed you both. You'll have to give me the details tomorrow when I come back." She'd avoided Jack's gaze while she hugged and kissed his sons, but now she said directly to him, "I didn't mean to ignore you, Jack. Did you have a good trip back?"

He was obviously trying to keep from smiling as he answered her. "It was the usual for this time of year. Too many semis going too fast and too many RVs going too slow."

"I prepped dinner for you—hamburgers, potato salad, corn, watermelon, and brownies. All you have to do is grill the burgers and corn." She turned toward the entryway. "Now that I've seen you guys, I'll head home and let the three of you enjoy your evening."

"NO!" came from both boys.

"You can't leave," Lucas said.

"You have to stay for dinner," Daniel added. "We have a surprise for you and Dad."

She caught Jack's eye, but he shrugged as if to say, "I have no idea."

"You just got home after being gone for two weeks. You should have family time with your dad."

Lucas said. "If you leave, you'll spoil the surprise. Dad, make her stay. Please?"

Jack ruffled Lucas's hair. "I can't force Quanna to stay, son, but if you two take your backpacks and duffels to your rooms, I'll see if I can change her mind."

The boys headed for the steps; Jack went into the kitchen; Quanna followed.

"Did you put them up to it?" she asked.

"No. It's completely on them. They've been going on about this surprise for most of the way home. I have no idea what they're talking about." He put his hands on her shoulders and touched his forehead to hers. "God, I want to kiss you so bad."

It was the answer she both wanted and dreaded. "We can't. Which is part of the reason I shouldn't stay for dinner. It'll only make it more difficult for both of us."

"You'll disappoint the boys if you go." He touched her face then ran his index finger over her lower lip. "Please, sweetheart. They have their hearts set on this."

"Uh ... Dad?" came from behind Jack.

Jack dropped his arms from her shoulders and backed away from her. "Daniel. What can I do for you, buddy?"

"We put our stuff in our rooms. Lucas is getting the surprise ready, and I'm helping set the table." He finally looked at Quanna. "Did Dad convince you to stay?"

She glanced at Jack and half smiled. "Yes, it looks like I'm having dinner with you."

"Okay. You and Dad can't go into the dining room. We'll carry the plates to the table when everything's ready. Then you can come in."

"Right." Jack turned to Quanna. "I guess we have our orders."

As soon as the burgers were cooked and the corn grilled, four plates were piled with food. Lucas and Daniel carried them, two at a time, to the table. Jack opened a beer for himself. Quanna poured lemonade for the boys and for herself and picked up the three glasses, ready to be led into the dining room for the big surprise.

At first, all she could see was the dinner she'd planned on a table set with familiar linens and dishes. Then she noticed a new addition. Above every placemat was a glass coaster. Each one was different, but somehow they all worked together as a set.

"The coasters are beautiful! Where did they come from?" she asked.

"We made them!" Lucas was bouncing up and down with uncontrolled glee.

"Your Aunt Amanda didn't tell me she let you work in her studio," Jack said. "Sam's wife is a glass artist," he explained to Quanna. "You're lucky guys," he added to his sons.

"She taught us all about glass and how to cut it and make designs with it," Daniel said. "It was awesome."

"I made mine and yours, Quanna. Daniel made his and Dad's. Aunt Amanda said they didn't have to be the same, but if we used the same colors, they would go together."

"This may be the nicest thing anyone has ever done for me," Quanna said as she sniffed back a tear.

"It's the best present you've ever made for me, for sure." Jack picked up the coaster at his place and examined it. "You did a great job. Thank you. And thank you for being thoughtful enough to make one for Quanna."

"It was my idea. I thought she'd like to have one for the nights she has dinner with us," Lucas said.

"And you were right. I do," she said.

"But you're crying," Lucas said.

"Sometimes people cry for reasons other than being sad. Sometimes it's when they feel emotional. Quanna's happy, I'm sure."

His words brought back their first night together with a gut punch. Quanna couldn't change the subject fast enough.

Dinner flew by as the adults were treated to a day-by-day recitation of what the boys had done while they were in Portland. It was mostly Lucas who did the talking, but Daniel provided key details, like the names of the horses they rode on the beach and the songs they heard at the Pink Martini concert.

When the meal was over and the boys had begun to load the dishwasher, Jack said, "Quanna, will you help me take a few cases of bottled water out to the refrigerator in the barn? I'll have crew here later this week, and I like to keep water there for them."

She nodded and picked up a case of twenty-four bottles and followed him out the mudroom door. When they got to the barn, he stowed the two cases he had carried into the refrigerator, took the one she'd brought out, and put it on a table. Then he led her to the back of the barn, drew her to him, and said, "I'm not sure I can do this, sweetheart."

She was afraid her heart would stop. "What do you mean?"

"This charade. I don't want to pretend you're nothing more than my kid wrangler. I want Daniel and Lucas to know what you mean to me. It's been killing me all evening."

"We have to be just boss and employee. At least for now. You agreed."

"Yeah, before I knew how difficult it would be." He brushed his mouth across hers. "Please tell me you're having as hard a time as I am."

Instead of words, she answered by putting her hand at the back of his neck and pressing her mouth to his. All the pain and passion, all the love she felt for him was in the kiss. She led the dance of lips and tongues this time, but he was a more than willing participant. When they broke apart, both of them were breathless. "Jesus, Quanna. I don't know how we'll get through this."

"We can if we want to."

"Give me something to look forward to, then."

"This weekend. I'm not working at the resort. Can you, I don't know, come have lunch with me one day?"

"Maybe I can do better than that. Barb was talking about one more camping trip with the kids before school starts, and this weekend was a possibility. If it works, will you spend the weekend here with me?"

The more time she spent with him, the deeper she would fall in love. She knew that. But she also knew she'd say yes to anything he asked her to do. So she said, "Of course I will."

On the walk from the barn to her car, they studiously avoided being close enough to touch, and when they both reached for the handle of the driver-side door at the same time and their hands brushed, they recoiled as if shocked.

She drove away, happy she didn't have to face the boys again, sure her mouth was swollen from Jack's kisses and her hair messy from his hands. With any luck, he would be so busy with his wheat for the next few weeks, she wouldn't see much of him around the house while she was working and wouldn't have to worry about a repeat of the scene in the barn.

Damn it.

•••

Jack watched her car trail dust up the hill to the road, trying to get his mind—and his body—calmed down before he went back to his sons. By the time he went inside, the dishes were done and Daniel was putting the placemats and new coasters away. Lucas had gone into the family room and had turned on the television after he'd completed his part of cleaning up.

"Thanks, Daniel," Jack said as he set up the coffeepot for the morning. "Good to see you guys haven't forgotten how to do your chores."

"We helped Sammy and Jack when we were at Uncle Sam's. Sammy and I usually did the kitchen cleanup while Jack and Lucas took care of Chihuly. I think Lucas wants a dog now."

"It wouldn't be the worst thing to have a dog around."

"We should ask Quanna about it first. Maybe she's allergic or something. And dogs are more responsibility."

"You're right. Before we decide to adopt a dog, we'll talk to her."

Daniel was quiet for a moment. "Dad, I was wondering something."

From the tone of his son's voice, Jack knew this was something important. "What is it, buddy?"

"You called Quanna 'sweetheart' when you were in the kitchen with her before dinner. I was wondering why."

"Did I? I guess I was trying to convince her to stay for dinner."

"Oh, is that why?"

Jack hated lying to his kids. But he had promised Quanna. "Well, you did ask me to get her to stay." For the first time he could remember, he couldn't look his son in the eye. "I wouldn't worry about it."

Daniel looked like he didn't quite believe it but said, "Okay, Dad. I won't."

Chapter 15

In spite of harvest, work schedules, kids, the annual influx of cowboys, tourists, and rodeo officials for the Pendleton Round-Up, and the other complications of their lives, Jack and Quanna managed to carve out time each week through the early fall to be together. On rare weekends, it worked out to be overnight. Often it was lunch on a Saturday. Jack grew more frustrated with keeping their relationship hidden as the weeks went on. It was particularly difficult now because he had time to spend with her. School had started for the boys, the cattle had been moved to their winter pasture, and his crops were all harvested. He was free for larger chunks of time to be in the house with her, if she'd let him.

But Quanna held tough on not mixing her job and their relationship. She wasn't being paid to be his mistress, she told him. "Then let's tell people we're a couple," he responded, "so I can see you outside work hours." But she couldn't agree to be open about their relationship. Not yet. He knew she was worried about gossip and understood she was concerned about her job. He tried to reassure her on both counts by promising her job was safe and repeating that no one would say anything snarky about his being with her. Nothing worked. He couldn't convince her to go public.

The way around her fear came to him while driving back from a two-day meeting with a Chinese trade delegation in Portland. Jack was so excited about it he raced his truck into the driveway and spewed gravel from his abrupt stop. It must have alerted Quanna to his arrival because she was standing in the open door when he got out of the truck.

Before she could say anything, he picked her up, whirled her around, and kissed her long and hard. "You have no idea how glad I am to see you," he said when he finally let her go.

"Wow. The meetings in Portland must have gone well."

"They did, but that's not important right now. I got home when I knew the boys would still be in school so I could talk to you about something."

"Now I'm curious. What's more important than a new trade deal with China?"

"I need something cold to drink, first." He took her hand and led her to the kitchen where he pulled a bottle of water from the refrigerator and took a long drink before offering it to her.

She sipped at it and handed it back.

"I got this great idea during the drive home. Would you be more comfortable talking here or in the living room?"

"I'm getting less curious and more nervous. Why do I have to be comfortable with what you're going to tell me?"

"Here or there, sweetheart?"

She walked to the living room and dropped into a chair. He followed and took the seat directly across from her. "Okay, you know I don't like skulking around. I want to be honest about us, go places in public with you. I hate feeling like I'm a teenager afraid to get caught out after curfew."

"And I keep telling you, some of your friends or family will say awful things about your dating an Indian."

"We've never come up with a way to prove or disprove your theory. Until now. I have a great idea. Besides swapping kids in the summer, one of the other traditions I let fall by the wayside when Paula was sick was the potluck we used to have here for the Civil War game. Most people I know went to either Oregon State or the University of Oregon and like to watch the annual football game between them. I used to host an inside tailgate party here. It's fun trash talking my friends and family members over a meaningless football game."

He got the laugh he hoped he would before continuing. "I want to do it again this year with you as my date. I called Sam and Barb from the road, and they're all for it."

"You started inviting people already? Without talking to me? And what about the boys?"

"I'd talk to them first. And Sam and Barb already know about us ..."

"Your brother knows? How? You never told me that."

"Barb called him when she saw you here."

"Crap."

"They're fine with it. Happy, in fact. So, my siblings know. I'll tell the boys we're dating today. We'll invite at most maybe two or three other couples who'll find out about us when they come to watch the football game. It'll be like a toe in the water." He grinned at her. "We get to leave the closet and have a great party celebrating our coming out."

"Toe in the water for you. Tidal wave for me." It took her so long to say the next sentence he was sure she was going to say no. "Okay. If that's what you want."

"We can tell the kids tonight at dinner and then ..."

"No, *we* aren't going to tell them anything. You're going to do it alone, after I leave. If they have any problems with it, they're more likely to tell you if I'm not here. You can tell me tomorrow how it turns out."

•••

Quanna wasn't eager to face the boys the next morning. Telling them about her relationship with their dad was a big step, one she'd fought for months. She wasn't exactly sure what she wanted before they went public—a shooting star, an alignment of the planets, a simple "I love you." Whatever it was, she hadn't gotten it. Instead, what she had was an impatient lover who wanted the world to know they were a couple. Now he was about to get his wish, starting with two young boys.

She was nervous about how it had been received. Suppose they'd been horrified when Jack told them? Hated the idea of their dad dating. Hated her for dating him. She'd hoped Jack would call her after he talked to the boys the night before, but he hadn't. Not that she'd been home. She'd had class, and if he'd tried to call, he wouldn't have reached her. Still, he could have left a message. But he hadn't. It made for a sleepless night.

When she let herself into the house, things seemed like the usual school day morning. The coffee was ready to turn on; there were sounds from upstairs of kids getting dressed. She busied herself getting out cereal bowls and boxes, pouring juice, and laying out silverware before packing lunches. The thumping of footsteps on the stairs told her at least one of the Richardson boys was on his way down to breakfast.

It was Lucas. "Quanna, can I have an extra cookie in my lunch? I promised to give one to my friend Mathias. He loves chocolate chip cookies."

"Good morning to you, too, Lucas."

He returned the greeting and repeated his question.

"What do you get in exchange?" she asked.

Guilt washed over his face. "Why do you think I'd get something for it?"

"Because you've never given a cookie away without getting something in return in the whole time I've known you. So, what're you getting for this one?"

"One of the pieces of candy his mom always packs for him."

"Then, actually you're just asking for an extra sweet, aren't you?"

"You weren't supposed to figure it out."

She corralled him in a hug and kissed him. "It's too easy to figure out your schemes when they involve sweets." She tucked another cookie into his lunch sack. "Okay, you can have an extra. But none after school."

"You're the best." Lucas grabbed the box of his favorite cereal and poured a huge amount into his bowl. "Dad told us you're his girlfriend now."

"Did he? What do you think about it?"

Around a mouthful of cereal and milk, he answered, "It's okay with me. Does that mean you're going to live here all the time?"

"No, why would I? I have my own home."

"There's a kid in my class. His mom has a boyfriend who lives with them. I thought maybe you would live with us."

"That's not the way we do things around here, buddy," Jack said from the doorway. He smiled and said, "Good morning, Quanna."

"Morning, Jack." She handed him his coffee and shook her head a bit to ward off any further conversation with him. When Lucas had gobbled down the last of his cereal and finished his juice, he hopped off the stool and ran to retrieve his backpack.

"How did it go last night?" she asked as soon as the boy disappeared up the stairs. "Lucas seems okay with it. How about Daniel?"

"He said he'd been worried because I was alone. He's happy I have someone to go out with." He brushed a wisp of hair off her forehead. "I told you. It's going to be fine."

"I hope so, Jack."

He topped off his coffee. "One thing I forgot about the Civil War party. While Barb and Amanda are here, we should start talking about Thanksgiving. My grandfather started the tradition of hosting a bunch of people for dinner to celebrate harvest and thank the people who made it possible. Thanksgiving's a bigger deal in my family than Christmas."

"How many people are you talking about?"

"Oh, thirty, thirty-five. Friends, family, the work crew. We provide the turkey and a couple side dishes. The appetizers, the rest of the sides, drinks, and desserts everyone else brings."

"*Only* turkey and side dishes? For thirty-five people? Are you kidding?"

"Makes the Civil War game party look easy, huh?"

Chapter 16

"Crap. Crap. Crap." Quanna pulled the pot of hard-cooked eggs off the stove, dropped it in the sink, and turned the cold water on full force. Not that all the cold water in the county would help. All the cooking water had evaporated because she hadn't been paying attention, and she was sure the eggs were ruined. It was just one more thing to go wrong this morning—the morning of the football game when she and Jack would be outed to his family and friends.

So far, she had spilled a box of cereal getting the kids fed, slopped coffee on herself, and broken a glass in the sink. Scrubbing the coffee from her jeans had diverted her attention from the eggs she was hard-boiling so she could devil them. Now the shells looked scorched, and she wasn't sure she could save more than a few. It made her want to cry.

"What's wrong, sweetheart?" Jack was setting up the bar in the family room and had come into the kitchen to collect the last of the glasses he needed.

"Nothing's going right this morning. I want everything to be perfect today, and nothing's even close." She fought tears back, not wanting to make the day even worse by having red eyes and a puffy face when their guests arrived.

"Everything is already perfect," Jack said as he wrapped her in a hug. "It's a beautiful fall day. The Beavs are predicted to beat the Ducks for the first time in about ten years. And, most importantly, you're here with me."

"But I was going to make deviled eggs, and I think I ruined them." She went back to the sink where the eggs were cooling, continuing her inspection.

He gestured in the general direction of the dining room. "You've already put out salsa and chips, pretzels and nuts, a cheese plate that could feed a small country, popcorn, cookies, and brownies, and if my nose is correct, you're cooking chili. With what our guests bring, I think we're good."

"I want it to be better than good. I want it to be ..."

"Yeah, I know ... perfect." He tipped up her chin. "You have that covered, too. I think you're perfect." He kissed her gently.

"I'm nervous about today."

"No. Really? I'd never have guessed." He snugged her hips against him where she could feel the beginning of an erection. "I might be able to come up with a way to relax you. It's been a while since we've been together so I can promise it won't take you away from your food obsession for too long." His smile was positively wicked.

Before she could respond, Lucas ran into the kitchen. "Aunt Amanda's car is coming down the road. Sammy and Jack are here!" Without waiting for a response, he raced to the front door, threw it open, and, as his father and Quanna watched from the kitchen, waved frantically, as if the driver might miss the house without his signal.

The arrival of Sam's family was quickly followed by the third Richardson sibling and her family. Barbara and Lane Benjamin had three boys—Wills, Andy, and George—who were in the same general age range as their two sets of Richardson cousins. Within minutes, the noise level was raised significantly as the seven boys, Sam's toddler daughter Kat, and his dog Chihuly took over the house, barn, and surrounding territory.

When two more couples arrived, the indoor tailgate party was complete. The Wilsons and the Ibarras were neighbors and were obviously, from the ease with which they greeted all the Richardsons, not to mention the gentle teasing and even the use of strange nicknames, longtime family friends. Quanna couldn't remember the last time she felt so out of the loop.

Saying she needed to check on the chili and cornbread, Quanna sought refuge in the kitchen. Were she to be honest, she'd confess she would rather be outside with the kids, who, in spite of the chilly weather, were playing some sort of game involving several kinds of balls with the apparent aim of keeping the balls out of Chihuly's mouth and putting them into a soccer goal net. She watched them for a few minutes, envying them their carefree game.

She was screwing her courage up to return to the family room when Amanda St. Clair, Sam's wife, came into the kitchen with a pile of dirty plates in her hands.

"I need a break from all the talk of wheat and cattle," she said. "Please tell me we can talk about something else out here. You'd think after being married to Sam for as long as I have, I'd have picked it up. But I haven't. Thank goodness he doesn't hold it against me."

"I can't imagine he'd hold it against you if you hated wheat and cattle."

Amanda laughed. "Any more than Jack would if you hated them."

Quanna could feel herself blushing. "I don't know if that's true."

"Oh, come on, he thinks you hung the moon. And it couldn't make us happier. He's taken care of everyone else for most of his life. It's long past time he gets to enjoy something for himself."

"I don't know what to say."

"You don't have to say anything. I can see you feel the same way about him." She put her hand on Quanna's arm. "Actually, I came out here to see how you're doing being dumped into the middle of this crowd. It intimidated me the first couple times, being the newbie in a group of people who had known each other forever."

"You were? I was afraid it was me."

"Nope. It took me a while to get comfortable. The thing is, they're great people. But they've been around each other so long they forget what it's like to be new to the group. And Jack probably won't figure it out unless you say something to him. Paula knew everyone from childhood on so he never had to worry about her feeling like an outsider."

Quanna let out a big breath. "Thank you. I wasn't sure I should mention it. I didn't want him to think I was complaining about his friends. Particularly after I told him I was worried about whether they'll think he's making a mistake because…well, you know."

"A mistake? Because you're younger than he is? I'm younger than Sam is, and no one said anything. Or are you worried because you work for him? Unless you're doing something horribly inappropriate in front of the kids—and we'd know because Lucas would rat you out in a New York minute—no one is going to ..."

"No, neither of those reasons. Don't you think there'll be people who'll say Jack's making a big mistake being with an Indian?"

"Why would anyone think that?"

"Because there are people who don't like Indians."

"I thought that attitude was long gone."

"It's not as obvious in the city. But around here, it still exists. It's more subtle than it used to be, according to my mom, but it hasn't gone away. I don't want people to think less of him because of who I am. Or have the kids bullied because of me."

"I had no idea. But I think you're safe here. I can't imagine anyone ever saying something nasty in this house."

"I hope you're right." Quanna didn't want to doubt Amanda, but she'd heard nasty comments in more places than she cared to count. And if Amanda didn't know there was still a problem with anti-Indian prejudice, then maybe she wouldn't know it if she did see it.

Quanna picked up a stack of clean plates. "I better get these out to the table. The game's starting soon, and I imagine there'll be a last-minute rush to stock up on food."

• • •

Jack waited until Quanna had left the kitchen before coming in from the living room where he'd been eavesdropping.

"Thanks for reassuring Quanna, Amanda. She's been so worried someone would make some crack about her being Indian, she hasn't wanted anyone to know about us. I had to work to convince her about today. Not that it's panned out the way I thought it would. She's been hiding in the kitchen most of the time pretending she's the help, not my date."

"She's worried about more than nasty comments. She's afraid your reputation will suffer. Or the boys will get bullied."

"I wouldn't worry about Daniel and Lucas. They have Indian classmates and teachers. It's no big deal for them. And I'm a big boy. I can take care of my reputation myself."

"Please, Jack, don't dismiss what she's concerned about. Take it seriously."

"I do. Of course I do. What I hoped she'd see today is how much my family and friends like her because she's a wonderful person."

"Not to mention she's made one of our favorite people happy."

He grinned. "It's obvious, isn't it? I'm happier than I've been in a long time."

Sam appeared in the doorway to the dining room. "Why are you chatting up my wife, brother, when you have a date waiting for you in the family room and the game's about to start?"

"Mostly because I knew it would annoy you," Jack responded. "But I've made my date wait long enough, I guess. So I'll give your wife back to you." He winked at Amanda. "No offense, sister-in-law."

"None taken. Let's go watch the game."

...

Five hours later, Jack and Quanna stood with their arms around each other, waving goodbye to the Wilsons and Ibarras as they left the ranch. All the guests were fed, half were happy with the results of the football game, invitations to have dinner before the holiday season set in had been extended to the couple, and the menu for Thanksgiving dinner had been settled. It had been, at least in Jack's opinion, a successful day.

As the last vehicle made its way up the dirt road, he leaned over and kissed Quanna before asking her the question he'd been dying to ask. "A good day, don't you think? The only thing I can think of to make it better would be if you could stay overnight."

"You know I can't. Besides, aren't you in mourning because OSU blew it in the last two minutes of the game? I don't think you'd be much fun tonight after the loss."

"Baby, I guarantee if I could have you in my bed, I'd be one hell of a lot of fun."

She made a cute, pouty face. "I'm sorry I won't get to find that out."

"Not half as sorry as I am." He took her hand, and they slowly walked back to the house. "But you didn't answer my question. Do you think it was a good day?"

"It was fun. Your friends were great."

"I told you they'd like you. All your worrying was a waste of energy." He stopped before they got to the front door. "So we have my family and friends out of the way. Now how about we tell your family? Should we have your mother and brothers here for dinner? Go to her house? What do you think?"

She groaned. "My family's complicated. Can we talk about it another time?"

"All right. As long as you promise we will talk about it."

"I promise but not right now. I need to get back into the house. I left Barbara and Amanda doing dishes and cleaning up the kitchen. I should be in there putting things away."

"Lane and Barb know where things go. And Sam's used to having Barb boss him around while Amanda laughs and enjoys the sight. It's part of the family ritual. You spent the week getting ready. Let them spend a couple hours cleaning up."

"I can't do that, Jack." She opened the front door and headed for the kitchen, which, to her surprise, was completely cleaned up. The only evidence of what had gone on was the sound of the dishwasher running and a stack of plastic containers on the counter: larger ones filled with chili, smaller ones full of cookies and brownies.

"I hope you don't mind," Barbara said. "There was a lot of chili left over so I'd like to take some home. Lane says it's the best he's ever had. And the boys have raved about your brownies and cookies since this summer."

"I'm taking some with me when we go home tomorrow, too, if you don't mind," Amanda said. "All I heard about when Sammy and Jack came back to Portland after their stay here was how good your cooking is. If you want to start a long-distance catering service, I'll sign up."

"I appreciate the compliments, but all it takes to please boys is to have a lot of whatever you're making. At least in my family. But take whatever you want. Jack and the boys will be living on the leftovers for a week if you don't."

Amanda dried her hands on a cotton dishtowel then asked, "Where do you want these dirty towels to go? "

"Leave them on the counter," Jack said. "I'll take them up to the laundry room when I take the boys up for bed." He looked back into the living room. "Where are they, by the way? It's alarmingly quiet around here."

Amanda said, "I sent them upstairs with ours already. They should be in pjs with their teeth brushed and reading. Or making a mess up there instead of down here. I'll go get them settled. You should take care of getting Quanna home."

"I have my car. I don't need a lift," Quanna said.

"But it's dark and looks like it's about to rain. You should have someone follow you home to make sure you don't have a problem on the road."

Sam said, "That doesn't make sense. Why should both of them drive all the way into Pendleton?"

Amanda stared at her husband. "Hush, Sam. I imagine your brother agrees with me, don't you, Jack?"

He grinned. "Yup. I absolutely do."

"Really, Jack, it's not necessary," Quanna said. "You have your family here. You don't need to ..." Apparently the expression on Amanda's face and Jack's grin registered. "Oh, I see."

"Good. Then get your things collected," Jack said. "You must be tired after all your hard work. I bet you can hardly wait to get into bed."

He may have been the only one who heard his brother say, "That makes two people in the room anxious for the pretty nanny to get into bed."

Jack ignored the comment. He merely said, "I'll go tell the boys what I'm doing, and then we'll hit the road."

• • •

"It's getting late. I don't want you to leave, but hadn't you better start back to the ranch?" Quanna had tried not to notice the clock, but the glowing numerals couldn't be avoided any longer.

"I don't want to leave, but I guess I have to." He sat up on the edge of the futon. "Before I go, is this a better time to ask about meeting your family?"

She sat up beside him, twisting the edge of the sheet in her hands. "This is as good a time as any, I guess. It's kind of a problem, introducing you to my family. Do you remember my telling you about what happened to my brother?"

"You mean his wife leaving him and their kids."

"Yes. She hated living on the reservation." She finally looked at Jack. "She's white. She moved back to someplace in the Puget Sound where she had relatives."

"You think it'll bother me in the same way? Is that what's worrying you?"

"No, I'm sure you'll be fine. It's my mom. She doesn't trust white people much because of what happened ... well, and a few other things over the years."

"So, all this about how my family would feel about you is what ... a reflection of the problems your brother had?"

"No, this is in addition to his experience. But since we've outed ourselves to your family, I guess we should do the same with mine. I don't know how my mother will react. She might even refuse to meet you."

Jack put his arm around her shoulders and pulled her into an embrace. "But she married someone who wasn't Indian."

"And it caused problems with her parents for years. Eventually, wanting to see the grandkids wore my grandmother down. But that doesn't mean my mother will just roll over about us. She accepted my brother's wife and got burned. I don't know if she'll be so accepting again."

"Okay, then, how do we get around it?"

"If we talked with my brother first, he might have some ideas. Maybe he'd even help us."

"Then let's set up something this coming week with him." He stood up, and put on his boxer briefs and jeans. As he was buttoning his shirt, he said, "Your brother's an artist, right?"

She tied the sash on her robe. "Yes, a photographer. Why?"

"Just refreshing my memory about him."

•••

Like hell he was refreshing his memory, Jack thought as he drove home through the fall rain. If it took winning over Quanna's brother to get help with her mother, maybe he knew a way to do it. He hoped his sister-in-law was still awake when he got home so he could talk to her. Or he would hit her up in the morning. Either way, she could be the key to getting Quanna's family to accept him.

Chapter 17

The following Wednesday, Jack and Quanna waited in the café at the Wildhorse Resort drinking coffee. At least, Jack was drinking coffee. Quanna was playing with her cup and looking around the room every few minutes wondering where her brother was.

He finally arrived, ten minutes late. Quanna was happy to see he was dressed in a neatly ironed shirt and a pair of new-looking jeans. Even though she knew he didn't dress in ratty clothes for work, still she'd worried about what he'd look like. She wanted him to make as good an impression on Jack as Jack's siblings had made on her.

"Sorry, Q. Got held up at the campgrounds with a customer. I tried calling you, but it went to voice mail." He put his hand out to Jack. "Hi, I'm Frank Morales. And you are ...?"

Jack took his hand. "Jack Richardson."

"Quanna's boss? Is there a problem?"

Jack glanced over at Quanna who shook her head before saying, "No, no problem. Not really. Why don't you order coffee before we get into what I want to talk about."

Frank ordered coffee. Quanna asked after her niece and nephew while they waited for it to arrive. After he had a chance to drink some of it, Frank asked, "So, ready to talk about why you wanted to meet this morning, Quanna?"

"Well," she began.

Jack interrupted. "Before we get to the reason we're here, I have something I want to give you." He dug in the pocket of his shearling coat and pulled out a business card. "This has the e-mail address of my sister-in-law, Amanda St. Clair, on it. She's a pretty well-known glass artist. If you'll send her images of your photographs and she likes what she sees, she'll pass them along to a gallery owner she knows in Portland who's looking for undiscovered artists to represent."

Frank looked down at the card then at his sister. "Did you put him up to this, Quanna?"

"This is the first I've heard about it. I'm as surprised as you are. When did this all happen, Jack?"

"We got talking last Sunday before she left to go back to Portland, and I mentioned Frank was a photographer with a good eye and she ..."

"How do you know I'm good?" Frank interrupted.

"I've seen your work in Quanna's apartment. Anyway, Amanda knows how hard it is to get started in the business and likes to help new artists. She also agrees with me that this side of the state should have more of a presence in the art galleries in Portland than it does. So, she wants to take a look at your work. You interested?"

"Interested? Of course I am. It could be a huge break." He turned the card over and over in his fingers. "But why are you doing this?"

"I like your work. In fact, I'd like a piece of it myself one of these days."

Frank looked back and forth from his sister to the man sitting next to her. Quanna could almost see the wheels turning in his head. "Is there a connection between what Quanna wants to talk about and this offer?" Quanna started to answer, but Frank waved her off. "No, wait. Let me see if I can connect the dots. You two are involved. Quanna's trying to figure out how to break it to our mom. She wants my help. Jack thought if he did me a favor, I'd be more likely to agree. Right?"

"Gee, I wonder why I even bothered to come along. I could have kept working while the two of you took care of everything." Quanna wasn't nervous anymore. She was annoyed.

"I apologize, sweetheart," Jack said as Frank said, "I'm sorry, Q."

"I don't know who's more annoying—Jack because you went behind my back to Amanda or Frank for not giving me a chance to explain what's going on."

"You're right. Let's start over," Frank said. He stood up and put his hand out to Jack. "Hi, I'm Frank Morales. And you are ...?"

"Sit down. Don't be absurd," Quanna said. She waited until he was settled back in his chair before continuing. "Okay. You're right. We're involved. And yes, I want to introduce Jack to Mom. And, yes, I'm looking for some advice on how to approach her."

Frank looked directly at Jack. "Was I also right about the reason you offered to help me get into a gallery in Portland?"

"I didn't think it would hurt." He reached for Quanna's hand, but she pulled it away. When Frank raised an eyebrow, Jack looked embarrassed. "I didn't tell Quanna so you wouldn't get mad at her if you were offended at what might be considered a bribe."

"Looks like you made the wrong Morales mad," Frank said. "I'll let you work it out with Quanna, but I'm not mad. I'd never turn down an offer of help. Your sister-in-law's right. Art is a hard business. But just so you know, I'd have been willing to help my sister even without the favor." He leaned across the table and swatted Quanna on the arm. "So if you can get over your snit about not knowing what Jack was up to, let's figure out how you approach Mom."

"If some of the conversation can include me from now on, I'm fine," Quanna said, not sure she felt fine at all.

"Okay, baby sister. I'll take your word for it. As for Mom, I guess the good news is she hasn't ranted about my ex-wife, the white devil, in at least a month. Maybe she's mellowing."

Jack shuddered. "It's that bad?"

"Yeah, but I'll talk to her. See if I can find out what her current mood is."

"Do you think we should invite her to Jack's for dinner or go to the house to see her?" Quanna asked.

"You definitely need to go to her. Making her come to you would be a bad move. And don't try to bribe her with flowers or candy, Jack. She hates that sort of thing, although if you brought a video for Miguel, it would be okay. Quanna's told you about our brother, hasn't she?" Jack nodded and he went on. "She'll expect you to answer a bunch of questions about your relationship. Be prepared for anything. Even with people she likes, she's blunt. Oh, and she has her heart set on Quanna graduating from college. You better be ready to tell her what you think about that."

"Not a problem. I completely agree."

"Good. She'll approve, at least of that response." Frank looked at his watch and finished his coffee. "Sorry to advise and run, but I gotta get back to work. We're unusually busy for this time of the year, and I'm short staffed. I'll talk to Mom and call you, Quanna. And, Jack, thanks for the contact with your sister-in-law. I'll follow up on it tonight."

He stood and pushed his chair under the table. Looking directly at Jack, he said, "There's one more thing, but it's not about Mom. If you hurt my sister in any way, any way at all, you'll have me to deal with no matter how many galleries you can get my work into. We clear about that?"

"Message received. And just so you know, you have an ally in my sister. She told me pretty much the same thing. Seems she likes Quanna better than she likes me."

"Sounds like your sister and I are on the same page."

•••

The ride from the resort to the freeway was quiet. So was the travel on I-84. When Jack turned off onto the road south, toward the ranch, he finally broke the silence. "Are you ever going to talk, or are we going to have to learn American Sign Language to communicate?" He thought the light tone of his comment would make her smile, at least, if not laugh. It didn't. "Come on, Quanna. Talk to me."

"I'm still mad."

"Yeah, I noticed. I've already apologized for not telling you I talked to Amanda. What else can I do?"

"I'm not mad about your talking to Amanda. Exactly."

"Then what is it—exactly?"

"You and Frank took over the conversation and moved ahead without me. I didn't even have a chance to explain to my own brother why I wanted to see him, much less discuss what would work with Mom. You made the deal with him to get a favor; then you and Frank worked it all out." She finally looked over at him. "It was like when you took on my neighbor or those jerks who were hassling me in the bar. Or when you announced we were hosting a party for the football game without talking to me. You had all the answers. I didn't have a chance to say anything."

"I didn't mean it like that. I thought I was helping."

"But you didn't ask if I wanted help; you assumed. You went ahead and made decisions for both of us without talking to me, without asking what I wanted you to do. If I wanted you to do anything at all."

He pulled the truck to the side of the road, shoved the gearshift into park, and turned off the ignition. "I'm sorry. Please don't be angry. I don't know what to say other than that. I guess I was doing what I would have with Paula. I grew up with the only other woman I've been with. I didn't have to ask her. I knew." He leaned over and kissed her forehead. "You and I are still learning about each other, and I'm obviously not always getting it right. Not yet, anyway. If I promise I won't make plans for the two of us without discussing it with you, will you cut me some slack while I figure it out? Please?"

The smile he had been waiting for finally appeared. "When you say it like that, how can I say no?"

He restarted the truck and got back on the road muttering, "Thank you, Lucas, for those lessons on begging and whining."

• • •

It took Frank less than a day to get back to Quanna to tell her their mother was receptive to meeting Jack. A time was set for the following Saturday afternoon.

Jack picked Quanna up at her apartment and, following her directions, drove to her mother's modest, one-story house back in the hills on the reservation. She was nervous for the whole drive, saying little. Jack occasionally patted her on the arm or the knee as reassurance but seemed to know not to say anything.

Frank answered the door when she knocked.

"You could have used your key, Quanna. This is your house, too," he said.

"I didn't want to assume," she said, after kissing him on the cheek. "This doesn't feel like the usual visit home."

Her mother appeared in the small entryway. "I'm glad to see you, Quanna." She kissed her daughter then eyed the man standing behind her. "Why don't you introduce me to your friend."

"Mom, this is Jack Richardson. Jack, my mother Winona Morales."

Jack extended his hand. "Thank you for inviting us, Mrs. Morales."

"Quanna doesn't need an invitation. This is her home."

"Of course. I meant ..."

Quanna interrupted. "Mom, could we all go in and sit down?"

Mrs. Morales led the way into a small living room and took her place in a brown recliner, back straight, legs at right angles and together, hands grasping the arm rests, a queen on her throne receiving her subjects.

Quanna sat on the flowered couch and patted the cushion beside her for Jack to join her. Frank dropped to the floor near the sofa and sat cross-legged, leaving a smaller upholstered chair empty.

It didn't stay empty for long. Quanna had already spotted her brother Miguel lurking in the hall leading to the house's three bedrooms. He came into the room after the others were settled and sat in the empty chair.

Quanna waved at him. "Hey, Miguel. There's someone here I'd like you to meet." She turned to her left. "This is my friend, Jack Richardson. Jack, this is my brother, Miguel."

"Hi," Jack said. "Nice to meet you."

"Did you bring me a present? Frank said you might bring me a present."

"Miguel, you know better than to ask something like that," his mother said.

"As a matter of fact, I do have something for you," Jack said. "Quanna told me you like cartoons. I got a couple new ones for you." He handed over the bag he'd been carrying. "If you already have these, I can exchange them."

Miguel pulled two DVDs out of the bag and grinned. "I like them."

"What do you say to Mr. Richardson?" Winona asked.

"Thank you." He was already leaving the room as he said it. "I can watch them by myself. In my room."

"Frank must have told you to do that," Winona said.

"He said you'd think candy or flowers would be a bribe to get you to like me, but some new DVDs for Miguel would be okay. My mother taught me to take something to a hostess when I visit so I was happy to have his advice."

By the way her mother fought to keep her mouth from curving up in a smile, Quanna knew Jack had scored a point or two for his honesty and his manners. She started to relax a little. Then her mother said, "Frank and Quanna, please go get the coffee and cookies from the kitchen."

It was impossible to say no when her mother gave a command. Quanna threw Jack what she hoped was an encouraging look over her shoulder and followed her brother. With luck, they could get it organized and out soon because she sure didn't want to leave Jack alone with her mother for long. Her stomach clenched when she saw the coffee hadn't been started, the cookies weren't plated, and the cups and spoons weren't out. Her mother had done it on purpose, she was sure, so she had time alone with Jack.

• • •

Jack didn't know how to start a conversation with someone he'd been warned might dislike him. He was trying to come up with something when Winona Morales surprised him.

"Thank you for what you did for Frank. I appreciate it. So does he."

"It was my pleasure. My brother's wife has been an advocate for emerging artists for as long as I've known her. She was only too happy to help."

"She liked Frank's work enough to pass it along to a gallery owner, he said. He got an e-mail from a woman who wants to talk about representing him."

"I'm glad it worked out."

"So, DVDs and introductions to gallery owners won over my sons. How did you win over my daughter? She's usually the levelheaded one."

The quick change of subject took Jack aback. "Ah ... I can't say I did anything deliberately. We just ... you know ... got to know each other and ... ah ... the longer I knew her, the more I came to care for her."

"How long has this been going on?"

"Since the late summer."

"Why has it taken you this long to tell her family?"

"We didn't tell anyone in either family until recently. We wanted to make sure we knew what the relationship was before we said anything, particularly to my kids. And Quanna's been afraid there would be gossip. I'm older than she is. She works for me ..."

"You're white and she's not."

"That concerns her, although I'm sure it won't be a problem."

"How do you know?"

"Because I know my family and friends."

He wasn't happy to see the unbelieving expression on Mrs. Morales's face.

"There will be gossip, I promise," she said. "Won't you get tired of hearing it? Maybe you should find someone more like you."

"You mean someone who's white." He leaned forward, resting his forearms on his thighs. "Mrs. Morales, in the years since my wife died, not once has a woman interested me in the least. Until Quanna. She's smart; she's beautiful. She brought music and laughter back into my home. My kids love her. My brother and sister love her. I don't share your fear that somehow it'll all disappear if some jackass makes a racist comment."

"So, you're serious about her."

"I love her."

"Enough to marry her?"

"We haven't gotten that far yet, but we're on the road."

"What about her education?"

"She needs to finish up her degree. She should be teaching a lot of people's children, not just mine. I've already told her I'll do whatever I can to support her education."

Winona Morales cocked her head and stared at him. She looked about to say something when Quanna and Frank reappeared, each carrying a wooden tray. One had four mugs of coffee on it, the other, sugar, milk, and a plate of cookies.

"Sorry it took so long. The coffee wasn't ready," Quanna said. From the worried look on her face, she was anxious to know what had gone on while she was in the kitchen.

Winona looked at her daughter. "Your friend doesn't pull punches, does he, Quanna?" She took a mug from the tray. "How do you take your coffee, Mr. Richardson?"

"It's Jack. And I like it black with two sugars, thanks."

She added sugar and handed him the mug. "Now, tell me about your boys. Quanna talks about them all the time when she visits. One's ten and the other's eight, if I remember right."

With that change of subject, the tension in the room seemed to lessen a bit as Jack and Quanna took turns telling Daniel and Lucas stories.

• • •

They hadn't been on the road more than two minutes when Quanna said, "Mom whispered 'he's no white devil, but you should be careful' when she kissed me good-bye. Which is high praise from her. What did you two talk about while we were in the kitchen?" Her curiosity had been close to overwhelming her ever since she'd brought the coffee into the living room.

"Weren't you eavesdropping?" Jack looked over at her and grinned. "I was sure you would be."

"Believe me, I tried. But with the noise the coffeepot made, Frank rambling on about the offer he got from that gallery owner, and Miguel's cartoon blaring, I couldn't hear anything but the occasional word, nothing like a whole sentence."

"It was an interesting cross-examination. She wanted to know how long we've been together, why we'd kept things secret." He kept his eyes firmly on the road when he added, "How serious I am about our relationship."

"What did you tell her?"

"Let's see, question number one, late summer. Number two, wanted to make sure we knew where we were headed." He stopped speaking, and her heart almost did the same, she swore. "Oh, yeah, and I told her I love you."

Quanna didn't respond, unable to dig words out to say anything without crying. Or laughing. Or both. Finally she drew herself together enough to say, "I think you should pull off the road."

He did as he'd been requested. "I probably shouldn't have said it to your mom before I said it to you, but it seemed like the right thing to do at the time."

Quanna flipped up the armrest between them, unsnapped her seat belt, slid over, and hopped onto his lap. "Shut up and kiss me, Jack."

He did that, too, as requested. The kiss was sweet and soft, gentle, and full of love. When it was over, she rested her head on his shoulder and played with his fingers. "Now, tell *me*."

"I never thought I'd say the words to another woman but I do, I love you."

"And I love you." She touched his face; he kissed her fingers. Nothing was said for a few moments as she continued to sit with her head tucked under his chin and he softly rubbed her back. "How soon do you have to pick up the boys?"

"Barb said she'd feed them dinner if we ran late. All I have to do is let her know."

"Make the call. And let's go to my place. There's a bottle of wine there with our name on it. I'm in the mood to celebrate."

Chapter 18

Preparing for the Richardson Thanksgiving celebration was much more involved than getting ready for the simpler celebrations Quanna was used to. This would be the first year since she returned from Portland that she would not be with her family for the holiday, and if she hadn't been so busy every day the week before the event, she might have been sad about that.

But there wasn't time to be sad. There was too much to do. She was surprised to discover that getting the food organized wasn't the most time-consuming or labor-intensive part of what had to be done. It was moving furniture around in the house to make room, then setting up the tables and chairs needed to seat thirty-two people. Not to mention getting the tablecloths ironed and the napkins sorted out and collecting the requisite place settings of china, silverware, and glasses—dozens of glasses. Most importantly, according to Daniel and Lucas, it involved making place cards and hollowing out the small pumpkins that would hold flowers and candles on the table, tasks which needed her supervision.

Starting the Monday before the holiday, people were in and out of the Richardson house delivering their nonfood contributions to the event. Luckily, everyone involved had participated before and knew exactly what to do and when to do it. If it had been up to Quanna alone to organize it, she'd have run for the hills by Tuesday noon and not come back until Christmas.

It was complicated enough organizing her part—the food. She arranged for pickup on Tuesday of the two huge turkeys and the ingredients for the side dishes she would prepare—green beans, mashed potatoes, and cornbread dressing. The next step was confirmation with the other guests that there would be sweet potatoes and cranberries, plenty of predinner nibbles, wine and sparkling cider, and pies of every sort from apple to pumpkin to pecan and at least two kinds of cheesecake.

She was so busy getting things ready for the big day she didn't have any time to worry about meeting a whole new set of Jack's friends.

On Thanksgiving Day, Quanna arrived at the ranch before Jack had made his usual 5:00 a.m. appearance so she could get the turkeys into the twin ovens. When he got downstairs, he distributed the place cards the boys had made while she finished setting the tables and placing the flower-and-candle-filled pumpkins in strategic places. Breakfast was at the kitchen island and was basic—toast, juice, and, for the adults, coffee. A lot of coffee.

It all went so smoothly, Quanna was able to relax for a few minutes and visit with Jack's siblings and their spouses when they got there early to lend a hand. She wasn't even nervous when the guests she didn't know began to arrive. Everything was on track to work out.

. . .

The adults were seated at a long line of tables running down the center of the dining room and, after a right angle turn, through the living room. The kids were at tables in the family room. It was noisy. It was frantic. It was the Thanksgiving of Jack's fondest memories, and he loved it. All the people who mattered to him were there.

He and Quanna sat at the junction of the line of tables from one room to the other where he always sat so he could see all his adult guests when he made his annual toast. As the platters of carved turkey were brought to the table, he stood and asked for everyone's attention. When there was enough quiet, he began.

"Here we are together again at the end of a busy harvest season, to give thanks for a pretty decent year. So, the first toast, as always, is to all of you, my friends and family. I'm grateful for all the hard work you put in every week of the year to ensure our mutual success." He raised his glass and took a sip. With big smiles and shouts of "cheers," the guests followed his lead.

"Next, I'd ask you to toast the people who helped put on the feast today. We're all thankful for what you brought for us to enjoy." Glasses were again raised and a few lucky cooks got kissed.

"Last, a special toast. Thanksgiving is my favorite holiday, as most of you know. But this year is more special than usual. Those of you who were here for the Civil War game a couple weeks ago got to meet a special woman. I hope you all get that privilege today." He turned to Quanna, sitting beside him, to direct his words to her. "This year, I'm thankful I have you to share this day with." He touched his glass to hers. "To Quanna."

He took a sip of wine, then kissed the top of her head before he sat down. "Okay, folks. Let's eat before it gets cold."

He noticed two things before he got caught up in passing the numerous serving dishes around. Quanna was wiping a tear from her eye, and Anne Salazar hadn't touched her wine for the last toast.

• • •

Dinner was over, at least the main course was. Parents had gone into the family room to see their kids; old friends were visiting with each other. It was the half-hour break needed before the dessert course appeared.

Barbara, Quanna, and Amanda cleared the dinner plates. Then Barb and Amanda went to check on their kids, promising to return when it was time to slice pies and cheesecakes. Quanna, who was to start the two huge urns of coffee perking, slipped out of the kitchen to the powder room off the mudroom while it was empty. She was washing her hands when she heard two male voices from the kitchen. One of them belonged to Jack. The other man didn't sound familiar; he did sound a little the worse for alcohol. She started out of the powder room but stopped when she heard the strange man say her name.

"What the hell is this with Quanna, Jack?" he said. "I mean, it's all well and good to invite an Indian to Thanksgiving. Hell, even the Pilgrims did. And maybe you could get a pass for hiring her. She probably works for less than a white woman would. But introducing her as your date is going too far. She's no good for you. You know that. They're all tramps. You'll be the laughing stock of the county."

"Lenny, you're drunk so I'm going to forget what you said. But you need to shut up. I won't have Quanna insulted in my house."

"It was Paula's home, too. What do you think your poor dead wife would say about this piece of Indian trash in charge of her kids? For all you know, she's stealing from you. And I'm sure she moved into your and Paula's bedroom, the little slut, where she plans on staying unless you wise up and kick her out. She knows a good thing when she sees it."

"I'll say this one last time—shut up or you have to leave."

"You can't throw me out. My wife is ..."

"Audrey is the only reason any of us tolerate you. But even she won't be able to protect you if you don't stop running on at the mouth about Quanna. I love her. She's a permanent part of my life now."

"You can't be serious. No one will have any respect for a guy who stoops to her level to get laid."

"That's it. You're out of here." He must have grabbed Lenny in some way because the next thing Quanna heard was a struggle in the small hallway leading from the kitchen to the back door. She stayed in the powder room, swallowing hard to calm her stomach, which was roiling from the tension she felt. She heard the back door close and Jack return to the kitchen. She knew she had to escape, to go someplace where she could get the ugly words out of her head, but her feet seemed frozen in place.

It was just as well she didn't move because the scene wasn't over. There was pounding on the back door. In a few minutes, Jack returned to the hall with a woman, apparently Lenny's wife. As they walked to the door, he told her what had happened, then asked her to take her husband home to sober up.

No sooner had the door closed again then there was yet another voice in the kitchen, trapping her even longer in the powder room. A woman's voice asked Jack what was going on. She sounded familiar, and when Jack said her name, Quanna realized why. It was Anne Salazar. Jack explained what had gone on with Lenny Dickson, not pulling any punches about the insults leveled at Quanna. She shuddered hearing the slurs for the second time.

Anne was quiet for a moment before saying, "You know I love you, Jack. And I want you to be happy. But I can't totally disagree with Lenny. He may have said it rather crudely, but I think on some level, he's right. I voiced my hesitation about hiring Quanna when you interviewed her. I haven't changed my mind. You need to find someone more ... more of our kind ... more like us."

"You mean someone white?"

Anne didn't respond, but she must have made some indication of agreement because Jack went on. "I can't believe what I'm hearing, Anne. Paula loved and respected her Indian pupils the same as her white pupils. Surely you knew that."

"Don't throw my daughter's opinions in my face. I knew her, too, and I doubt this ... this *arrangement* is what she had in mind for her sons or her husband after she was gone." Her tone softened, became almost wheedling. "You know I only want what's best for you and the boys. But I don't think Quanna meets the criteria."

"I, and Daniel and Lucas, respectfully disagree with you."

"How can you be sure about the kind of influence she'll have on your boys? What do you know about her background, her family, her education?"

"I know more than you do. I've met her family. I've seen her work with the boys doing homework—hers and theirs—and I've seen the good grades the kids are getting after the nosedive they took when Paula died. She's the best thing that's happened to all three of us in a long time." His voice was getting harsh and strained. "If you feel so strongly about Quanna, maybe you'll feel more comfortable not coming to see the boys here."

"You wouldn't dare keep me from seeing my only grandchildren." Her voice had anger in it.

"No, I wouldn't. But I also won't force Quanna to deal with someone who clearly doesn't respect her. When you want to see the boys, we'll make arrangements for them to come to you."

Anne made a noise like a strangled cry.

"Look, let's not make this any worse than it is right now," Jack said. "Come back into the living room. We'll talk about this later when we've both had a chance to think about it a little more."

Stunned into inaction by what she'd overhead, Quanna wasn't sure how long she waited before peeking out of the powder room to make sure no one was in the kitchen. Jack and Anne were gone, but now Barbara and Amanda were there. They'd begun to cut pies and cheesecakes into slices, chatting, apparently oblivious to what had gone on before they arrived.

Unfortunately, Quanna was not.

After all the promises and reassurances she'd gotten about how nothing offensive would be said about her in this house or by Jack's family or friends, she had heard the kind of ugly words she had feared she would. Because of who she was, Jack and the boys would suffer. It was exactly like she'd told him it would be.

And now she had to decide what to do. Should she pretend she hadn't heard? Wait to see if Jack told her about the conversation? Act as if everything was fine until he did?

Well, it wasn't fine, and she couldn't pretend.

What she could do was run. Luckily she had hung her coat and purse in the mudroom when she'd arrived so she grabbed them and ran out the back door to her car, praying it hadn't been blocked in by someone else's vehicle.

It took some maneuvering, but after a few minutes, she managed to get out of the yard full of cars and pickups and was up the driveway on her way home, away from the ugly words now rattling around in her head, words which had made this the worst holiday of her life, which woke her up from her dream world to the nightmare she had been afraid was always there. She'd have to leave the Richardson Ranch permanently. Had to protect the man she loved, the kids she loved, from what was just under the surface of Jack's world.

It was the only thing to do even though it meant her plans for graduating from college were once again on hold. She'd be back to square one, forced to move into her childhood home so the little money she made at the resort could go to her mother.

And today she was supposed to be thankful? For what?

• • •

Jack saw his sister waving from the kitchen, clearly trying to get his attention. He was still seething from the last time he'd been in that room and wasn't anxious to return, but Barbara looked determined.

"What's up, Barb?"

"I think Quanna just left. Did you send her someplace to get something?"

"No, she should be around here. She was going to start the coffee." He realized what he had said and what must have happened. "Shit." He went into the mudroom and saw her purse and coat were gone. "Goddamn son of a bitch. She was in the back hall and heard."

"Heard what?"

"Lenny Dickson calling her an Indian tramp and Anne Salazar agreeing."

"I'm not surprised at Lenny. He'll say anything when he's drunk. But Anne? What got into her?" Barbara asked.

"I don't know, but I have to go after Quanna." He glanced outside. "My truck's blocked in. Can I borrow yours, Barb?"

"Of course. My purse is in the front hall. I'll go get the keys. But what should we tell people?"

"Tell them Quanna felt sick, and I'm making sure she's okay. Can you ...?"

Amanda shooed him out the back door. "Go around and meet Barbara outside the front door so you don't have to answer a lot of questions. Don't worry about anything here. Go find out what's going on. Tell her we're worried about her."

•••

"Quanna? Sweetheart? I know you're in there. Open the door so we can talk."

She'd ignored the initial knocks on the door, figuring it was Jack, knowing she didn't want to talk to him, hoping he'd go away. But now he was making so much noise her neighbor would be sure to come out into the hall.

She opened the door. "I don't want to talk to you right now."

He stepped inside before she had a chance to close the door. "Talking's exactly what we need to do." He reached for her, but she avoided his embrace.

"Please. Don't."

"I know what you overheard. And I'm sorry you had to be subjected to such garbage. But, sweetheart, Lenny's a drunk and an ass. We only put up with him because we've known his wife all our lives."

"And Anne? Do you just 'put up' with her?"

"I can't explain what she said. It shocked me. But you can't take what you heard to mean everyone feels that way."

"It was bound to happen. I was foolish enough to believe you when you said it wouldn't because I wanted so much for it to be true. But it isn't. What happened today is what's true." She swallowed hard and put on her most determined face. "So, I have to stop living in my dream world. It'll never work out between us because of people like Anne and your friend. That's reality."

"You think ignorant comments will change the way we feel about each other?"

"What I know is those kinds of comments will ruin your reputation and make it hard on the boys, which is what I've been trying to avoid. We can't go on like this. Not now that I know ... we know ... what I was afraid of was there, under the surface, all along."

"This doesn't have to change anything. We can work it out. I know we can."

"And I'm afraid of what will happen if we try, Jack."

"Please don't make this decision in the heat of the moment. Take the weekend. Think about it. Then on Monday when you come to work, we can talk about it after the boys are in school. Talk about how we're going to deal with it."

"We deal with it by facing facts. Like you said once, you need to know when to move on. And we've arrived there. We can't be involved, can't see each other again or be part of each other's lives."

"What exactly do you mean by 'can't be involved'?"

"It means what I said. A clean break. Not seeing each other anymore. It means I can't work for you, either. Not after what's gone on between us. I'll come back to work next week and continue in my job until you find a replacement."

"You're dumping Daniel and Lucas, as well as me? They'll be devastated."

"Don't play that card. It's hitting below the belt."

"Not when it's the truth. What am I supposed to tell them?"

"Nothing. I'll talk to them. I'll tell them I have a chance to finish school so I can teach. It's not altogether a lie. I've saved enough money to go to school almost full time next year, and I think I've worked out a way to get my degree without having to move back to Portland. I'll tell them I can still see them on weekends. It's not as if I'm going to disappear and never see them again."

"There has to be another way, Quanna. I love you. I don't want to lose you. Please think about it before you make a decision affecting us all."

"I won't be the reason people think badly of you. Or the reason the boys are humiliated and bullied in school. This is for the best. For all of us."

He tried to put his arms around her again, but once more, she backed away. "Don't. You know that'll make it more difficult for both of us."

"What's making it difficult is what you're determined to do."

"Please, Jack, go back to your guests. I'll see you Monday when I come to work."

"Will you think about this over the weekend so we can talk next week?"

"I'm not going to change my mind."

He opened the door, but stood there for a second or so before saying, "And I'm not either. I love you. Nothing will change that."

Chapter 19

"Are you mad at us?" His voice trembling, Lucas sounded as if he were close to tears. Quanna hadn't heard him come into the kitchen where she was packing the usual Monday lunches for him and his brother.

"No, sweetie, I'm not mad at you. Why do you think I am?"

"You left on Thanksgiving without saying good-bye. You didn't even have dessert. And you didn't come back on Friday. Aunt Amanda and Aunt Barbara said they didn't know why you left, and Dad won't tell us anything."

"I'm sorry I upset you. But I'm not mad." She wiped her hands on her jeans legs. "I do have something to tell you when Daniel comes down."

"He's in the family room. I'll go get him."

A few minutes later, two pairs of brown eyes were looking up at her, one set begging the news not be bad. The other pair guarded, as if knowing it would be.

"I told your dad this already. Now I have to tell you. I'm going to stop being your nanny. I've been working a long time to finish college so I can teach. And I think I can in the next two terms. I'm going to try. But I can't take that many classes and still work here. So, I'm leaving as soon as your dad finds someone to take my place."

Lucas threw himself at her, clutching her around the waist. "You can't leave. We love you."

"I'm not going to disappear. I can see you on weekends, if it's okay with your dad and works out with your schedules."

"But it won't be the same." Lucas was now verging on a full-fledged meltdown.

Daniel stared hard at her. "Will you still be Dad's girlfriend?"

Quanna shook her head. "I think it would be better if I wasn't." She put her hand on his shoulder. He shook it off.

"Don't you love Dad anymore?" he asked.

She had hoped she could get through the week without any more tears, but it was beginning to look like she wouldn't. "Sometimes, Daniel, love isn't enough."

"That's not what our mom said. She used to sing a song about all you need is love."

"It's a good song and I wish it were true, but it's not." She peeled Lucas off with a hug and a kiss. "You better get your stuff for school. You have to be ready when your ride gets here."

"I'm their ride this week." Jack was standing just outside the kitchen. She wasn't sure how much he'd heard of their conversation, but from the look on his face, he'd heard enough of it to make him unhappy. He made for the coffeepot, giving her and his almost tearful son a wide berth. "And I'll be picking them up, too. You won't have to be here for them after school this week. You can leave early."

"If you want me to, I will."

"There's not much around here of what I want lately. Only what I have to deal with." He poured coffee into a travel mug and took the sugar bowl she handed him. "Get your backpacks and coats and let's go, guys. We have a couple other kids to pick up."

• • •

Quanna wasn't sure Jack would come back in the house after he dropped off the boys at school. But he did. He came in through the mudroom and stopped at the door to the kitchen, staring at her, saying nothing.

"Is there something you want?" she asked.

"You made Daniel and Lucas unhappy this morning." He was standing with legs apart, his shoulders squared, twirling his ring of keys. "Is that what you were going for? If you were, congratulations. You succeeded."

"You know it's not. I said I would tell them I was leaving, and I did."

"You broke their hearts."

"Stop. Please stop." She could feel the tears begin to leak out of her eyes. She'd done little else but cry for four days. How was it possible there were any more tears left?

Before she could move, he was holding her, rubbing her back, making soft, reassuring sounds against her hair. It was so tempting to melt into him, let him comfort her, but she couldn't. If she did, all the resolve she had worked to acquire over the weekend would be gone. She jerked away from him. "I can't ... I mean, you shouldn't ... we can't ..."

"Yes, we can. You know we can."

"What I know is what I heard right here in this kitchen four days ago. And I won't subject you and the boys to any more of it. A lifetime of hearing ugly things like that would be far more painful than a momentary sadness because I'm leaving."

"A *momentary sadness*? Is that what you think of my feelings for you?"

"I didn't mean you. I meant the boys."

"You underestimate how important you've become to them. And you're avoiding the question about how I feel about you."

"How we feel won't begin to stand up to how the bigots feel. Believe me. I know how ugly it can get."

"Is this about what happened with your brother and his wife?"

"No, of course not. She didn't like living on the rez. It's not the same as you being hurt, the boys being hurt, by nasty gossip because of who I am. Of what I can't change, don't want to change even if I could. This is about what I've been telling you all along would happen as soon as people found out you were dating an Indian." She wanted him to understand, to believe the truth of what she was saying, to see reality.

But he seemed unimpressed. He stared at her. Finally he broke eye contact, tossed his keys into the bowl on the counter, and shed his coat. "We keep going around and around the same circle. I don't seem able to make you hear what I'm trying to say. If you won't change your mind, I guess I might as well give up."

He hung up his coat and, his back to her, said, "I'll be taking the boys to school and picking them up this week. You won't have to be here for them after school. You can leave any time you want. I won't be here during the day so make sure you lock up when you leave."

Turning to face her, he added, "One last thing before I go. Aren't you doing the same thing you were angry about that day we met with your brother? Making decisions for both of us without talking it over with me? Is it any fairer now than it was then?"

"This is entirely different."

"Is it?"

Before she could explain how different it was, he was out of the kitchen and up the stairs. He stayed in his office behind a closed door, and she didn't see him again until he left to pick up the kids at school.

• • •

True to his word, she didn't see him any of the following days except for a few minutes in the morning before he took off to drive the kids to school. The rest of the day, he was gone. She missed him. She found herself preparing dinners she knew he liked, making the desserts he favored. Even going into his bathroom to smell his sage soap.

She was torturing herself, she knew. But she needed to have some tiny contact with him. Although it made her sad, she wanted to save those last few memories for when she wouldn't have any contact at all.

On Thursday morning, when Daniel picked up his lunch after breakfast, he asked, "Did you mean it when you said you would come see us on the weekend when you weren't working?"

"Of course I did."

"How about this Saturday? We need a ride to a soccer game. I heard Dad say he wouldn't be here."

"Okay. I'd be happy to give you a ride. Where's the game and what time does it start?"

"I think it's in Pendleton. And if you're here before ten, it should work out."

It seemed an odd way to phrase it, but feeling guilty about hurting him by leaving, she agreed.

Chapter 20

Quanna was packing up her apartment, a box a day, preparing to move. She'd given two weeks notice to the building manager the day after Thanksgiving. With her full-time job about to end and not wanting to touch the savings she had so carefully accumulated to pay for classes winter term, she was resigned to moving back to the reservation. Although her mother had been gracious and hadn't asked any questions when Quanna had called to see if she could have her old bedroom back, it was a far from ideal move. But she hoped it was temporary.

On Thursday evening, she was filling a box with the contents of a kitchen cabinet when there was a knock at the door. Fearing it was Jack coming to try once more to persuade her not to leave, she didn't answer at first. Then a woman's voice said, "Quanna? Are you there?"

Curious, she opened the door a bit. It was Anne Salazar.

"Oh, good. I'm glad you're here. I was afraid you might be out or working at the restaurant. I would have called in advance, but I wasn't sure you'd say yes to seeing me so I took a chance and came to see you." She took a breath. "Sorry. Didn't mean to ramble on. I'm a little nervous. Can I come in?"

"I guess." Quanna opened the door enough to let her in.

"Are you moving someplace?" Anne said, looking around at the boxes.

"In a couple weeks, I'll be moving in with my mother." She was in no mood to go into details so she changed the subject. "What can I do for you, Anne?"

"You can hear me out while I try to explain my part in the embarrassing fiasco on Thanksgiving. I won't try to excuse myself. What I said, what I did, was inexcusable. But I would like to explain it." She sank onto the futon. "Could I bother you for a glass of water?"

Quanna went to the kitchen and took her time putting ice then water in a glass, trying to figure out how Anne could possibly make what happened on Thanksgiving understandable. She brought the glass to her visitor and took a seat on the small rocker, waiting to hear what the woman had to say.

Anne took a long swallow of water, put the glass down on the table next to the futon, and began. "Maybe I should start with a little background. I'm not sure if you knew this, but Paula—the boys' mother—was my only child. When she died, I wanted to curl up and die, too. There didn't seem to be any reason to live. I don't know what I would have done if Jack hadn't asked me to help with the boys. I grabbed onto his request like a lifeline. It felt like I was getting another chance to be with Paula. At least, with the part of her still here—her sons."

Anne was twisting her wedding ring on her finger as she continued. "Having to quit taking care of them was like losing her all over again. When Jack started to interview my replacement, I realized my role in raising them really was over."

She sipped more water. "Before the day you came to the ranch, I had only seen one of the other applicants, and she was older than I am. So I was surprised when you came to the door for your interview. I didn't expect someone so pretty, so enthusiastic, so ... so young. It got worse when the boys got home. I could see from the first time you met them how they reacted, especially Lucas. I knew it wouldn't take long before they loved you. And they did. Then Jack fell in love with you, too. They were all moving on, leaving Paula behind, and I was still stuck in the same place without my daughter and now without the only thing left of her."

No matter how hurt Quanna had felt from the words she'd overheard Anne say at the ranch, it was impossible not to feel sympathy for her. "Oh, Anne, Daniel and Lucas would never change the way they feel about you ..." Quanna began.

"Please. Let me get this out before I lose my nerve." Anne finished off the glass of water. "All our friends loved you. All I heard from them was how happy they were for Jack. How wonderful you were with the boys. Everyone was so busy liking you, no one stopped to think about Paula. You were taking her place, and I hated it. Jealousy ate at me."

She sighed. "I was a stupid, jealous old woman who, after two glasses of wine on Thanksgiving, said horrible things about another human being who didn't deserve any of it. When I heard what Lenny had said, I thought maybe I could dislodge you from the ranch by agreeing with him, even though I knew every word I said about you—every word he'd said—was untrue. You'd think that knowing Jack as well as I do, I'd have known he'd never listen to that sort of garbage. I guess I was just that desperate." She picked up the glass again, only to discover it was empty and put it back down.

"I have spent the past week regretting every single word I said on Thanksgiving and trying to get up enough nerve to come here to apologize. I can't imagine you'll forgive me and I'm sure you're angry, but I hope you'll find it in your heart not to take it out on Jack and the boys. They love you. They don't deserve to be hurt because of me."

Quanna didn't say anything. Couldn't say anything, she was so stunned by Anne's words.

Anne started to rise from the futon. "There. I've said my piece. I'll leave you ..."

"No, wait." Quanna swallowed hard to compose herself. "You don't know how much it means to me to have you come here. Thank you. Both for the apology and the explanation. I never thought about what you must have gone through when Paula died. I can't imagine what it must be like to lose a daughter, although I know a bit from what Jack and the boys have said about what it was like for them to lose a wife and mother."

"They talk about Paula to you?"

"Of course they do. So do Barbara and Amanda and Sam. No one's leaving her behind, especially Jack and the boys. Daniel wants to make sure Lucas has clear memories of her so he tells him stories about the things they did as a family. And Jack ... Paula was part of his life from the time they were kids. How could you ever think he'd forget her? He'll always love her."

Anne began to weep softly. Quanna went to the kitchen for tissues, which she shared with her because she, too, was tearing up. "Paula is part of them, part of their lives. No one can change that. No one wants to change that, especially me. You have no reason to be jealous."

The two women almost simultaneously wiped their eyes and blew their noses. Anne had a weak smile on her face as she said, "I didn't expect you to be so understanding. You're as wonderful as Jack says you are." She blew her nose again. "So, if you're okay with me now and if you know Lenny Dickson has been banned forever from the Richardson Ranch, can things go back to the way they were with you and Jack before Thanksgiving?"

Quanna shook her head. "As much as I appreciate your coming here and what you said, I don't think going back is possible. Thanksgiving showed me what I'd been afraid of all along—there are people around who don't like the idea of a white man being with an Indian. I can't set Jack and the boys up for that kind of treatment."

"Oh, you're doing it for Jack and the boys."

"Of course I am. Who else would I be doing it for?"

Anne finally stood. "Well, it occurs to me you might not be protecting Jack as much as you're protecting yourself. I wouldn't have thought you would be afraid of anything, but giving up because of what might happen ..."

"Anne, this is about *knowing* what will happen, not worrying it might. I want to spare Jack and the boys having to go through what I'm sure they'll have to face because of who I am."

"If you say so." Anne put out her hand. "I don't have the right to ask to be your friend. But I do hope you can overlook my recent behavior and give me another chance to win your regard."

Quanna shook her hand. "Absolutely. Thank you again. I appreciate your honesty and your courage in coming here." She opened the door.

Anne paused in the doorway. "Quanna, we're all afraid sometimes. I was afraid to come here to see you. Courage isn't feeling no fear. It's facing the fear and moving ahead in spite of it. If you don't want to take advice from me, I understand. But you might want to think about what I just said. It applies to you as much as it does to me." This time her smile was open, friendly, and honest. "I hope I see you again."

Chapter 21

During the drive out to the ranch on Saturday, Quanna kept hearing Anne's words. Was she giving in to fear as Anne had said? And was she being honest about what she was afraid of? And for whom?

And then there was Jack's accusation. She *had* made the decision to break things off without talking to him. Was it because she was being brave for him or because she was being afraid for herself?

She didn't have the answers, but she acknowledged she had to talk to Jack in order to try to find them. She'd think about it over the weekend, and maybe by next week, she'd have the courage to do something about it.

Her plan to wait until the following week changed abruptly when she arrived at the house and saw Jack's pickup in front, in its usual spot. Maybe fate was suggesting rather strongly now was better than later.

She parked next to it and tapped her fingers on the steering wheel for a few moments trying to decide if she wanted to go in. When Anne's final comment resurfaced again in her mind, she decided to take the advice and a first step by facing *all* the Richardsons.

Daniel answered her knock on the door. "How come you didn't use your key?" he asked.

"I'm not coming to work today, am I? And it's not my house." She stepped into the familiar entryway, looking around for evidence of the owner of the truck. "Your dad's pickup is out front. I thought you said he wasn't here this morning."

Daniel avoided her gaze and shifted his weight from one foot to the other. "I guess I misunderstood."

"Daniel." She used the tone of voice that always got him to do what she asked.

"Okay. I guess I knew he would be here."

"So, what about getting to the soccer game?"

"There isn't one. I wanted you to come here when you weren't working and Dad was here so you could talk and make everything all right again." He looked so unhappy she wanted to hug him. "But it didn't work. He went riding. I tried to get him to stay, but I couldn't."

"He didn't want to see me?" Maybe her bravery was already too late.

"I didn't tell him you were coming. I told him we needed him here for homework and stuff. He said he'd help when he got back. He's been riding a lot this week. To think, he says."

"You shouldn't have lied to me, Daniel. You could have asked me to come talk to your dad."

"I didn't know if you would say yes."

He had her, and he probably knew it. "I don't know what I would have said. But I never had the chance to decide, did I?"

"Please. Wait for him now."

The last thing she wanted was to have a conversation with Jack—this conversation in particular—within earshot of two curious kids. "Maybe I can go to him if you know where he went."

"I think he goes out to the pond where the cattle are."

"Oh. Then I guess I can't. I don't know how to find the road there."

"But you know how to get there on a horse, don't you?"

• • •

Jack had been pitching stones into the pond for who knows how long, trying to decide if he was going to finally do what he'd set out each morning that week to do. On one hand, it made sense to get rid of the reminders of his hopes for a life with Quanna. On the other hand, if he did what he'd planned, it would be a sign any future with her was definitely off the table. Was he ready to give up? God knows, there had been little indication his tiny shred of hope was warranted. But there was still a part of him desperate to hang on to any possibility no matter how infinitesimal.

He was about to reach into his pocket for the offending items when he heard the sound of an approaching horse. Damn it, Daniel had disobeyed again. He whirled around and started to light into his son. "How many times have I told you ..."

It wasn't Daniel. Twenty feet away from him was Quanna. On Rose.

"You're not Daniel," was all he could think of to say.

"No, I'm not." She dismounted and led the horse toward him.

"And you're riding Rose."

"Daniel saddled her for me."

He had to smile. "The devious little ..."

"You don't know the half of it. He asked me to come out to the ranch today to take him to a soccer game because you were busy with something else."

"What soccer game?"

"Exactly."

She was now so close he could reach out and touch her. He didn't because he was sure she'd back away, but knowing he could made his heart ache with need. "What are you doing here?" His tone was more demanding than it should be, but he needed to know what was going on.

"Like I said, I was lured here by a ten-year-old." She seemed to be looking any place but at him.

"I didn't mean here as in the ranch. I meant here as in this spot."

"Oh, that. Well, I had decided on the drive out here I needed the answer to a couple of questions. And I can't answer them without talking to you. Besides, I owe you the truth about something. Since Daniel set it up so nicely for us to be together, I'm taking advantage of it."

"What questions do you need answered?"

"Do you think I'm a coward?"

"Of course not. Why would you even ask?"

"Anne pretty much called me one, and I'm beginning to think she was right."

"Anne Salazar? That's terrible. When?"

"When she came to apologize on Thursday, she said I wasn't trying to protect you and the boys. I was afraid and trying to protect myself. I told her she was wrong. But the more I thought about it, the more I realized how right she was."

She looked directly at him for the first time. "I kept saying I was trying to keep you from being hurt by what people like that Lenny guy would say. But it's not true. I was scared. Gossip is like water falling on a rock. At first it rolls right off. But eventually, the incessant drip, drip, drip begins to make an impression. After a while, it wears away the rock completely."

She touched him for the first time, placing her hand in his. He regretted the gloves he was wearing kept him from skin-to-skin contact with her.

"I love you so much I couldn't run the risk you'd turn away from me because of the comments I knew people would make. It would kill me to lose you because of who I am. So I took the coward's way out ..."

"And sent me away because you were afraid I'd walk away." He finally understood what had happened. The relief he felt must surely show on his face. It definitely showed in his shaking hands as he took both of hers. "I thought you knew me better, Quanna. I love you. You have to believe me. The opinions of some racist jackass could never change that. I'm not like your brother's wife. I'd never walk away because things got a little complicated. Life's complicated. I know that better than most. You don't just give up. You keep going."

"Maybe my brother's experience was more on my mind that I was willing to admit. Maybe that's what made me so scared." She shivered, and he drew her closer. "I thought I was the brave one in this relationship because I was willing to face the truth about what people might say and you weren't. But I'm beginning to believe you've been the brave one all along." She shivered again. "Sorry. It's freezing out here."

Unbuttoning his shearling coat, he wrapped it around her. Her cold hands shocked him when she put her arms around his middle. "Oh, sweetheart. We need to get you home and in front of a fire."

"Let me finish first before we have two eager eavesdroppers. There's another question. You said I was doing the same thing I accused you of doing—making decisions for us, for all of us, without consulting anyone else. Okay, then let me ask you, if you don't think we should break up because of what happened on Thanksgiving, how do you think we should handle stuff like that? Because, trust me, it won't be the last time."

"About that. I owe you an apology. I didn't take it seriously when you warned me there were people like Lenny among my friends. I'm sorry. I won't make that mistake again. But what do I think we should do? Act as a team. Present a united family front. Call the bigots out about their prejudice when we hear it. Talk to the kids so they're not blindsided in case it happens to them. Live our lives without giving those assholes space in our heads."

"You mean it, don't you?"

"Of course I do." He kissed the top of her head. "As long as we're together, we're strong enough to face anything. I'm sure of it."

"There's one last thing."

"Right, the truth you think you owe me. You've got me curious."

"I got the job with you under false pretenses. I took down almost all the fliers you put up so I wouldn't have too much competition because I wanted the job so badly."

For the first time in a week, Jack laughed. "That's not much of a lie. But at least it explains why so few people contacted me. This time, there have been a dozen or more."

"Have you already hired someone?" She sounded worried about the possibility. Which made him happy.

"Not yet. I haven't even scheduled interviews. Thought I might get to it next week. Or the week after. I figured if I put it off long enough, I might have a chance to convince you to stay."

"Now I see where Daniel gets his deviousness."

"Speaking of the conniver-in-chief, we should get back to the house. I don't like to leave them to their own devices too long. And you're turning into an ice cube."

"Why are you out here in this weather, anyway?"

"I was about to do something drastic." He pulled two rings from his coat pocket. "I was going to pitch these into the pond so I wouldn't have to look at them every day. Think I'll keep them now." He held out his hand so she could see them. "Amanda brought them on Thanksgiving. A jewelry designer she knows made them for me. I wanted rings with a special meaning for us. So the designer braided metals to remind me of how you wear your hair and used copper, silver, and gold to represent the strands that make up the two of us. They're meant to be our wedding rings. I was going to ask you to marry me before you left on Thanksgiving."

Her smile was tenuous, struggling as she was to overcome the tears backing up in her eyes. "They're beautiful," she managed to get out.

"Pretty enough to make you say 'yes'?"

"To marrying you? If I'm forgiven."

"I think we've established we both need forgiveness. So, if we've agreed to that, is your answer 'yes' for sure?"

"Absolutely yes."

"Then I can finally do this." The kiss to seal their engagement was sweet, if a bit salty from her tears. "I've missed that for the past week. But since I can't warm up the rest of you right now, let's get you home," he said when the kiss ended.

"And give Daniel a chance to gloat."

"I'm not sure I want to give him the power. But it'll be hard to avoid."

"Should you tell them we're engaged or should I?"

"First one back to the house gets to. And just so you know, Hero always beats Rose."

Hero didn't win this time. It was a tie. However, there was no need to decide who would tell the boys. Apparently, when Daniel and Lucas saw the couple walk hand in hand from the barn after they put the horses up, it did the trick. At least, from the smiles on their faces, it seemed the message had been received: Quanna was back. For good.

A Sneak Peek from Crimson Romance
The Gift of Love by Peggy Bird

The last thing Isabella Rodriguez wanted for her birthday was a book on how to find herself. The accompanying condescending remark from her oldest brother Luis about how she was wasting her life and needed to read the book, and the nods of agreement from her three other brothers, made it worse. She wanted to throw them—and their gift—out of the house.

She tried to lower her blood pressure and calm her anger by taking a few cleansing breaths. Unfortunately, what was effective in her yoga class didn't seem to work anyplace else, so she gave up the attempt and let her emotions win. "I don't need anyone's advice on how to live my life, Luis. Especially not yours." She was sure steam was coming out of her ears.

Luis continued as if he hadn't noticed anything—the words, the tone, or the steam. "Look, Izzy, it's not just me. All four of us agree. We love you. But you've been living for free in Dad's house ever since he died while the rest of us cover the taxes and the cost of keeping it maintained. The house was left to all of us, not only to you. Those of us with families would rather support our kids, not our sister. I don't know if we're more frustrated or worried that you seem hell bent on living like some trust fund kid on our mutual inheritance but—"

"My name is Isabella," she interrupted. "Bella, if you must shorten it. Never Izzy, in spite of your continued use of the horrible sounding name. And I'm twenty-seven, not a kid."

"Okay, whatever, *Bella*," Luis said, his hand slicing the air in an impatient gesture. "But your name was all I got wrong. The rest is dead on. You haven't had a serious job since you left California. It's like you just stopped living when you moved to Portland." He ran his fingers through his mop of curls, one of the few traits Bella and all her brothers shared. "God knows we've tried to help. How many contacts did we give you in the real estate business here? Contacts who might have had a job for you."

"I didn't realize pressuring me to take the jobs in the family business no one else wanted was help. Or trying to set me up with a job I didn't want. I thought it was just interference. As this is."

Luis ignored her comment and went on with his lecture. "You shouldn't bear *all* the blame for where you are in life. Mom and Dad indulged you because you were their baby girl. But Mom and Dad are gone. It's time to get over being spoiled by them."

The mention of her parents punched her in the gut. As the only girl, the youngest in the family, and a late in life surprise for her parents, she'd had a special closeness with them both. And taking care of them in the last years of their lives had only strengthened an already strong relationship. Especially with her father, who'd had a particular soft spot for her. The empty space left by his death the year before was a lot smaller now than it had been right after he died, but it was still there. She missed him. Badly. No more so than today, her birthday.

If he'd been alive, this would have been a joyous celebration. He loved throwing parties for his kids, even when they were grown up. When her four brothers had said they'd all be bringing their families up from California for her birthday, Bella had visions of a family reunion and a party close to what her father would have arranged. It was serendipitous her birthday fell on a Friday this year, making it possible for them to all make it to Portland in time for dinner and, she had hoped, a weekend together. Friday the thirteenth of July would be her lucky day, she thought.

Except it hadn't turned out at all as she'd expected. Her celebration, it seemed, had merely provided an excuse to call a meeting to handle a crisis—her. She should have known. The four men never all came to Portland for anything other than a family matter to take care of. A new roof for the house. Papers to be signed for the business. Their father's funeral. She was in the same category as home repairs and memorial services. She hadn't figured it out until her three sisters-in-law took their kids and hightailed it out the door right after eating the dinner she'd carefully prepared for everyone. Leaving their gifts for her to open without them, they made no excuses and didn't say goodbye. They waited until she was in the kitchen after clearing the table and left, abandoning her to the mercy of her brothers.

What a stupid fool she had been to actually think her siblings cared about her birthday. All they cared about was their own agenda.

At least Luis had brought up the subject of her future after the women and children had hit the lifeboats for the safety of the shore. Or wherever they were headed. The *one* good thing about all of this was that he'd had the courtesy not to embarrass her in front of her nieces and nephews.

Luis glanced over at her second oldest brother Ernesto, a signal to run with the conversational ball, apparently. Great. They were tag-teaming her. She wondered if they'd scripted in advance what they were saying.

"It's time we stop paying for you to have a carefree life, Izzy," Ernesto said. "Most of us have families, kids to support. We want to sell the house so we can finally get our part of the estate."

"Still Isabella. Still not Izzy."

"Jesus, Izzy, is that all you get out of this conversation? We use a nickname you've never liked?" Carlos, the next brother in the lineup, chimed in.

"What I'm getting from this conversation is that you four, as usual, are making decisions that affect me without any consideration of what I might want."

Luis looked like he was about to interrupt and bring the conversation back his way, but she wasn't going to let him. "You had your say, brother. Now it's my turn." She raised her eyes to meet his gaze so directly she swore he flinched. Good. Maybe he finally saw how angry she was.

"I have done everything this family has ever asked of me. When I graduated from college, I went into the family real estate office like I was expected—no, *ordered*—to do. I didn't complain. Instead, I worked my way up from receptionist to running the place. But you couldn't let me enjoy my success for long, could you? I was told to move to Portland to take care of Mom and Dad. I didn't object even though I had friends and a life in California." Her hands fisted with the anger she still felt from having it all yanked out from under her when, two years before, her mother had been diagnosed with cancer and her aging father had been unable to manage her care. Because she was the only girl, she was expected to take care of her parents. So she met her obligation like the good daughter she was.

From the sideways glances Luis and Carlos exchanged, she knew she'd hit a nerve. "I'm an equal part of this family, and I don't deserve to be talked to like this." She turned to Javier, the brother closest to her in age and affection, who was sitting beside her on the couch. He looked uncomfortable, like he wasn't happy with how the conversation was going. "Javier, how could you do this to me on my birthday?"

"I'm sorry, Bella," Javier said. "We probably should have picked another time. But we've been talking about it for weeks, and since we're all here ..." He let his words trail off and shrugged. "We thought it would be better to tell you in person, and who knows when we'll all be together again." He tried to put his arm around her shoulders, but she scooted over to avoid the hug.

"We need to get this taken care of," Luis went on. "The real estate market's recovered; houses are selling; it's time. Besides, don't you want something better for yourself? From what I can see, all you do is rattle around in a big house, writing short stories you can't get published while you study off and on for a real estate broker's license."

Before she could respond, Javier added, "A broker's license I don't think you ever really cared about getting." Over her weak attempt to ward him off, he took her hand and squeezed it. "I'm right, aren't I? You really don't want to get into the real estate business, do you?"

As much as she resented having to admit one of the brothers was right about anything, Javier was correct. She had only said she'd study for the test because she thought the family wanted her to. It had never been her idea to become a real estate broker.

"Look, whatever-your-name-is," Luis said, "you did a great job running the office in California, and we all agree you were amazing taking care of Mom and Dad. I don't know what we'd have done without you. But that was then. This is now. We need to close out the estate. And the truth is, the fat bank account Dad left you when he died is getting low. You don't have to go back to the family business if you don't want to. But you do have to find something you want to do that makes you enough money to support yourself in a place of your own. That's reality. You can't afford to keep this house going, and we don't want to do it anymore."

"If Dad were still alive, you wouldn't dare do this to me." She knew she was tearing up, but she was determined not to cry in front of them.

"If Dad were still alive, we wouldn't have to do this. But he's not. And we do. End of story." Standing in front of her, Luis tried to pull her up from the couch. "Don't be angry, Isabella. We're only trying to do what's best for all of us." He, too, reached to put an arm around her. "Give me a hug to show me you understand."

She refused his hand and his hug, standing without his help. Drawing up to the full extent of her five foot two inch height, she glared at him and stuck out her chin. "What I understand is this is a hell of a way to wish me happy birthday." She picked up several empty coffee cups from the cocktail table in front of her. "All right. If you all agree it's time to sell the house, I guess I'm outvoted. Put the house on the market. If that's what you came for, you have it. Now I think it's time you all left. Until it's sold, this is still my home. So I have the right to have whom I want here, especially on my birthday. And right now, that doesn't include any of you. Go back to your families and your expensive houses and luxury cars and leave me alone." She was tired of the discussion, tired of trying to fight the inevitable. She only wanted them to be gone so she could mourn the end of yet another phase of her life brought on by the demands of her family.

Luis shrugged and, after trying one more time to kiss her goodbye, headed for the door accompanied by Carlos. Ernesto patted her on the arm before he joined them. Javier stayed behind, looking even more uncomfortable than he had before. "I'm sorry. I wish there were ..." he began but didn't seem to know how to finish. Instead, he changed the subject. "How about I stay and help clean up?"

"No, it's okay. I can do it myself. And don't worry about the others. I've been steamrolled by those three more times than you've had hot meals. I'm used to it."

She turned so he wouldn't see the tears beginning to fall and escaped to the kitchen. In a few minutes, she heard the click of the deadlock indicating Javier had left and locked up after himself.

Two hours later, Bella had run a couple loads in the dishwasher, bundled up the tablecloth and napkins for the laundry, and swept up the cookie crumbs her nieces and nephews seemed to have deposited in every room on the first floor. Pouring herself the last of the wine from dinner, she settled in the living room again, surrounded by her father's books, art glass, and the plants she struggled to keep alive only because he'd loved them so much. She tried not to replay the conversation she'd had with her brothers, but it was hard not to.

The worst part was she knew in her heart, no matter how mean it was of them to spring it on her at her birthday dinner, they were correct—it *was* time to sell the house. She might not want to join the family business, but she knew enough about it to understand they needed to take advantage of the improved real estate market.

Which meant she had to do what she'd been avoiding ever since her father had died—figure out what was next for her.

Luis accused her of having no focus. That wasn't true. She'd always had focus. Granted, it hadn't been on her own dreams and ambitions. Instead she'd concentrated on what her family wanted her to do. Ever since she'd been a kid, she'd tried to be the perfect daughter. She listened to her parents. Didn't cause any trouble. Didn't object when the rules for her brothers were different from the rules for her. Gritted her teeth when her father—and often the oldest of her brothers—cross-examined her friends like a prosecutor in a high-profile criminal case. She knew how much her father adored her. Knew he was going to those extremes to do what he thought would protect her. She never complained. At least, not to him. She understood that her father and, later, her brothers were overprotective because she was the baby of the family, a status she seemed doomed never to outgrow.

And, no, she hadn't pursued her interests. She'd listened to her parents when they said her writing would never pay the bills. Instead, she got the business degree the family wanted from the college the family insisted she attend so she could work in the home office of the family real estate business. Like the family wanted.

True, in return for doing what her parents asked her to do, she'd been protected her whole life. Her father had cosigned for her car loan. Her mother slipped her extra money every now and then.

And when she moved to Portland, they completely supported her in exchange for her taking care of them.

When her father died, she lost more than her last parent. She lost her moorings, the sense of security they'd given her. It had upset her so much that she'd done a couple foolish things in the months following his death. She'd spent more money than she should have on new clothes, for one. Worse, in a desperate attempt to keep from having to worry about any of the messy details of carving out a life of her own, she'd tried to latch on to a family friend in the hope he would marry her. Thank God Marius Hernandez had been in love with someone else, which saved her from the terrible mistake of marrying someone she didn't love solely for the security of being taken care of.

After her aborted plan to seduce Marius into marrying her blew up in a very public and embarrassing scene at the Portland Art Museum in front of half the art lovers in the city—and the woman Marius loved—she'd almost been frozen in place, unable to decide how to head her life in a direction that would make her happy. In the past year, she'd only made two decisions of any note. First, she decided to stay in Oregon out of her brothers' reach so they wouldn't be able to "help" her anymore. The scene after her birthday dinner showed how well *that* decision had worked out.

The second decision had been more successful, however. She'd gotten a part-time job, which she loved, with an interesting company run by a woman named Summer Olsen. Maybe that was a place to start. She could ask Summer to help her with her decision. A decision that would be based on what she wanted, not on what her family expected. This time, she'd make a plan for her life based on her goals and ambitions. As soon as she figured out what they were.

Somewhere, under the layers of the "good daughter" who'd been there for years, was a woman who had dreams and desires, just like everyone else. All she had to do was drill down deep enough to find her. And she'd better do it fast. The house wouldn't take long to sell.

• • •

To fast-track the beginning of her new life, Bella turned to her boss, the owner of "Break Up or Make Up"—or as everyone called it, BU/MU (pronounced Boo-Moo). The firm offered counseling, group sessions, legal advice, and practical assistance to people who were trying to fix broken relationships, either personal or professional. The founder, Summer Olsen, and Darcy Ross, a combination office manager and writer, were the only full-time staff. But the roster of consulting psychologists, social workers trained in counseling, and lawyers, all of whom worked with clients on a contract basis, was extensive. There were also writers available to ghost letters from clients to about-to-be-ex business partners or lovers when clients couldn't or didn't want to do it on their own. Bella had been one of those writers for almost two years, gradually moving from a few hours a month to what was now a half-time job. In spite of what her brother assumed, it paid rather nicely.

Bella and Summer had scheduled lunch the Monday after Bella's family dinner to celebrate her birthday. It was the perfect opportunity for her to pick her boss's brain about ideas for what she could do or people she should talk to who could help her figure things out. Summer knew everyone in Portland worth knowing and would be only too happy to help, Bella was sure.

When she arrived at the BU/MU office, the very pregnant Darcy greeted her with a birthday card and a hug made awkward by her belly before waving Bella into the boss's office.

"Happy birthday, sunshine," Summer said, barely glancing up from her computer. "Give me a few minutes to finish up what I'm doing here, and I'll be ready to take you out for a birthday lunch." When she looked up to get a response, she frowned and looked over the tops of her red-framed reading glasses. "Sorry. I guess I should say, happy birthday, raincloud. What's up?"

So much for putting on a good face.

Bella shook her head, then nodded before shaking her head again.

"Good to see you're clear about what the problem is. Want to talk about it?"

"I planned to wait until lunch to talk to you, but maybe it would be better to get it off my chest now. Mind if I take the victim's chair?" Bella dropped into the seat in front of Summer's desk where her clients usually sat.

"You know I don't like to call my clients victims. Well, not most of them. What's going on?"

"My brothers announced at my birthday party on Friday they're selling my house—my dad's—*our* dad's—house. And they told me I'm a spoiled brat who needs to grow up and find herself."

"Ouch. Happy birthday from your loving family."

"Yeah, well, the truth is, however angry they made me by bringing it up on my birthday, they're sort of right. I haven't really gotten things together in the year since my dad died. I've let it slide because I could. And now I'm not sure how to start. I haven't really had a lot of practice setting goals for myself. In the past, my goals have been dictated by what my family wanted."

"I thought you wanted to write."

"Okay, let me be more specific: I haven't figured out what I want to do to make enough money to support myself. Writing fiction sure hasn't done that and won't for the foreseeable future. The payments for the dozen or so pieces I've had published barely cover the cost of gas for my car for a month. And even if I finish editing one of the novels I have drafted and get lucky enough to find a publisher, I'm not well known enough to make much money at it." She waved a hand helplessly in frustration.

"I'm sorry you had such a rotten birthday dinner. What do you need to cheer you up?"

"Actually, I need more than cheering up; I need advice. I was going to ask you if you could help."

Summer had been sitting back in her chair with a funny look on her face. Now she took her glasses off and leaned forward on her elbows, staring across the desk for a few moments before saying, "Actually I might be able to give you more than advice."

Still lost in the memory of her disastrous birthday party, Bella didn't pick up on Summer's subtle change of subject at first. "If you have some ideas about a career counselor or someone else I could talk to, please, feel free to give me some recommendations. I'm totally at sea about what to do next. But whatever it is, I have to do it soon because I'm pretty sure the house will move quickly in the current market."

"I'd be happy to recommend a counselor if you still want one after I tell you about my idea." Summer picked up a yellow legal pad, then flipped it back onto her desk. "I've spent the last couple days trying to write a job description for an ad to find someone to manage this place while Darcy is on her six-month maternity leave. She's due at the end of September, and I need to find someone soon so I can get her—or him—trained before she leaves. But the more I tried to describe who I was looking for, the more I became convinced I was going about it the wrong way. You could be the answer to my problem."

"If you need help writing the job description or the ad, I'd be glad to draft it for you. Just tell me what you're looking for."

"I'm not suggesting you write the copy; I'm suggesting you take the job."

Too stunned to answer for a few moments, Bella searched her friend's face expecting to see a "gotcha" look or a smirk. Instead, Summer's face seemed to say she meant it. "Why would you want to hire me?"

"Playing down your abilities is not exactly how you get a job, girlfriend." Summer tore several sheets of paper off the pad and crumpled them up. "If I'd thought of this days ago, I could have saved myself the struggle of trying to describe what I was looking for. All along, I've been looking for you."

"Me? How do I qualify for the job?"

"Well, I want someone with experience managing an office—and from the way you've described your family's real estate business in California, you were in charge of an operation a lot bigger than this one. Next, I want someone who's a good writer—which you've certainly shown you are." She lobbed the paper wad into the recycling basket. "And I want someone who knows what we do and is enthusiastic about doing it. Again, you fit the description."

"Are you sure?"

"Absolutely. Don't you see? We can solve each other's problem. Working for me for six months will give you time to get your feet on the ground and figure out what you want to do next. And hiring you means I won't have to go through the trauma of finding and training someone new for only a short time. Or, even worse, hiring people from a temp service who won't be able to do what I need done. And I won't have to get used to having someone strange in my office every day. I already like having you around. It's a classic win-win."

Bella agreed with much of what Summer had said. She understood and supported what Summer was trying to do with her business. And the two women not only got along but also worked well with each other. They'd met at a City Club of Portland lunch. Bella had been there to connect with someone her brother Luis had wanted her to get to know. Summer had been there to pass out her business cards to people at the lunch table. The guy never showed up, but the two women had clicked.

It was a big leap from part-time writer and friend to full-time office manager, though.

"It's simple: I need you and you need me."

"If I said yes, what would you be willing to pay?" Bella asked.

"Exactly what I pay Darcy: $4,000 a month plus medical and dental. Does that cover what it would cost to rent an apartment and keep your little bit of metal you call a car on the road?"

"I think so. Plus I still have some savings from what my father left me." She closed her eyes as she realized, for the first time since her birthday dinner, she felt hopeful. "Okay. I'm in. Where do I sign?"

"Think about it while we have lunch. We can talk contract when we get back." Summer stood up and grabbed her purse. "Let's blow this popsicle stand. I'm starving."

"All of a sudden, so am I," Bella said.

Maybe, she thought as they walked toward Twenty-First Avenue, this wasn't the worst birthday of her life after all.

For more from Peggy Bird, check out:

A Holiday for Love series:

Sparked by Love

Praise for *Sparked by Love:*

"With lies and hidden agendas, you have to wait and see till the very end for all the pieces to fall together!" —Chicks That Read

"A warm, fuzzy romance read. Leo and Shannon are just so sweet together. There is plenty of steam as well. Very enjoyable read for romance lovers." —Wilovebooks, 4 stars

"This book had the Triple 'S' factor for me: short, sweet and sexy . . . a wonderful book." —Red's Hot Reads, 4 stars

"This was my first time reading Peggy Bird. I was pleasantly surprised by not only her writing style, which was very engaging and flowed, but also her characters." —Book Nerd, 4 stars

Unmasking Love

Praise for *Unmasking Love:*

"Spicy and modernized, this story relies on the mystique and romance of Romeo and Juliet, without the bad ending. Peggy Bird brings heat and heart to Halloween." —4 stars, I Am, Indeed

"I love the author's witty writing style, which is present right from the opening lines of this book. Ms. Bird successfully builds deliciously, believable sexual tension between Julie and Trace; you can almost hear the cracks of electricity!"—5 stars, Ellesea Loves Reading

"The story isn't long, but it wasn't rushed. ... Beautifully written and wonderfully engaging."—4 stars, Written Love Reviews

Lights, Latkes, and Love

Ringing in Love

Second Chances series:

Beginning Again

Praise for *Beginning Again*:

"Both Liz and Collins are great characters. Liz is not a bitter middle aged woman, but instead a very strong and brave lady. I really enjoyed *Beginning Again* because it was an easy read that made my gray autumn day a little bit less gray." —Long & Short Reviews

Loving Again

Together Again

Praise for *Together Again*:

"...a very enjoyable romance. I loved the main characters and the great writing. I always admire strong, independent women, so if you also enjoy those qualities in a heroine, and enjoy a well-written romance, I recommend this one." —Night Owl Reviews

Trusting Again

Praise for *Trusting Again*:

"The book moves along at a nice pace and the characters are believable and realistic. It is a well-written story with a wonderful ending!" —Harlequin Junkie

Believing Again

Falling Again

In the mood for more Crimson Romance?
Check out *Art of Affection by Ellen Butler*
at *CrimsonRomance.com.*

www.ingramcontent.com/pod-product-compliance
Lightning Source LLC
Chambersburg PA
CBHW010309100726
47905CB00011B/3268